THE

BIG

BOOK OF

SOUNDS

AND

OTHER

STORIES

THE

BIG

BOOK OF

SOUNDS

AND

OTHER

Jon Steinhagen

STORIES

Black
Lawrence
Press

Black Lawrence Press

www.blacklawrence.com

Executive Editor: Diane Goettel
Book and cover design: Amy Freels

Published 2016 by Black Lawrence Press.
Printed in the United States.

Contents

The Wind Catalog

 # 41—A gentle, late spring wafting with overtones of 2 AM on the stretch of grass adjacent to the University library one block from your dormitory, coupled with a suggestion of someone you finally managed to sit with and say nothing to and hold. Vintage 1990.

As with anything new and unfathomable, they did not know what to do with the Wind Catalog except laugh at it. While they laughed, a new and updated Wind Catalog arrived. Some of them looked through this one and only laughed in smaller portions at the empty illustrations coupled with neat call letters and elegant descriptions.

 # 103—A slight, early summer breeze with hints of caramel corn and cotton candy and grease from the axles of small rides quickly constructed and then taken down at weekend's end in the parking lot of the local supermarket every October. Vintage 1979.

They discover that the Wind Catalog is distributed by the Classic Wind Consortium. There is a website. When they check the website they discover it is a reproduction of the catalog only with an easy-to-use navigation bar and a prominent link to JUST ADDED.

The Classic Wind Consortium lists no address. It lists no CEO or founder. Visitors to the site are assured that sales representatives are standing by to take their orders when a 1-800 number is dialed. They dial, curious. They dial because it won't cost anything. A pleasant sales representative answers. No one knows what to do next. Did they really need vintage wind?

 # 57-58—Squall. One of our most popular items. For our Down East customers now displaced, who miss the thrill of life on a fishing boat. Chilly and briny, in two sizes. Vintage 1948.

They agreed the Wind Catalog was an elaborate hoax. They discussed it over their mochas and tofu wraps and during their poker games and church breakfasts. It is impossible to capture and store wind. It is impossible to enslave a gust and keep it on a shelf for a generation or longer. It is impossible to keep a large supply of anything that rushes invisibly, regardless of how keenly it is felt and remembered by the skin. It is impossible to hold and sequester and market and ship and disperse the most fleeting, temporary, and ephemeral element. Air. Not just air but air in motion. Wind is horizontal. Drafts are vertical. Air that carries where it has been and who it has seen. It is not possible. However.

 # 144—A dry and desolate puff across the desert, hot and bold, popular with our customers poor of complexion and meditative of spirit. You'll feel the relentless iron sun with this classic. Vintage 1925.

And yet, they reasoned, if the Wind Catalog is not a hoax and to be believed, it stands that someone had achieved the impossible.

A way had been found to preserve, to harvest, to save, to classify, and to vend the winds of the past. Not only had this been done, but someone had been doing it for a very long time.

 # 410—The Battle of Bunker Hill. No further description needed. Delivered in a fingernail vial. Limited supply. For serious collectors. Market price.

They took to wondering what the market price of the wind from the Battle of Bunker Hill would be. They took to wondering how such a thing as a market price for wind could exist. They continued to ignore the Wind Catalog's second edition, no matter how disturbed and curious they were. Some of them had spoken of actually spending a few dollars to order something and see what would be delivered and how. They wanted to see the instructions. They wanted to learn a new language. Wind reactivation? Would a special machine be needed? There is always a need for a special machine. That's how they make their money.

 # 212a—A healthy gust for the first kite of the season, redolent of the dense woods surrounding the hill upon which the kite mingles with other kites, with just a hint of fresh dogwood and deer; your father is with you. Vintage 1965.

A man named Hellison orders a #35.

 # 35—A strong lakeside zephyr, northerly, fresh with midnight and prom corsages and charter boat thrusting through the dark waves. On the cold side; give her your coat. Vintage 1987.

Hellison tells no one, not even his wife. Hellison waits. Hellison has second thoughts about blowing twenty-five bucks on what is obviously a hoax. Hellison waits. Hellison is home when the box is delivered. Hellison is surprised to read the simple instructions: Place this canister in the corner of the room in which you wish to experience it, open it, sit down, close your eyes, and enjoy.

Hellison goes to the guest bedroom he used to use as a study until he discovered he had nothing to study and puts the canister in the corner, opens it, sits, and closes his eyes.

The six of them are emerging from the limousine and are walking down the stone staircase to the river and there is so much wonder in the city tonight and everything is all set and another six are meeting them and how grown-up it is to be tuxedoed and shiny and sharp and the girls looking like elegant Christmas gifts and Sharon is never letting herself be not arm in arm with him and her dress is strapless and her shoulders are smooth and this is the well he's lost count time she's kissed him tonight with her mouth open and all of them are boarding the boat and how rich they feel how elegant and special and rare and no one can stop talking all of us all of us boys are self-conscious we pat our moussed hair and tug at the sharp starchy points of our dress shirts and the girls are as inviting as pillows with satin covers and the boat churns into the Chicago River and the buildings the grand places of living and working reach for the black sky and there is a feeling of I Want This I Want This Always and we glide under the Michigan Avenue Bridge and midnight people wave to us and yes we are special and rare and wonderful and we are out on the lake bobbling along in freedom and release from the land and all of us all six couples maybe seven are finding private spots along the rail and looking out looking out and it is all dark and behind us now the city look-

ing like a land of amusement parks and Sharon is kissing me or maybe I am kissing her oh no this is a mutual kiss these are mutual kisses and they are long and warm and she shudders and my coat is off and around her shoulders and that makes her want me even more and the boat is silent except for the engine pushing us through the black mysterious water along the shore and then soon too soon back to the river and up the stone steps and back into the waiting limousine and back to the expressway and back to our suburb and back to our houses dropped off one by one by one and no reason to think of that now because out here with Sharon in my coat pressed against me and nothing but lips and necks and searching hands and the waves and the endless darkness of the water and the sky and we are special I am special I am rare I Want This Always.

The canister empties. Hellison opens his eyes. Hellison hears a quiet house, sees a dusty sunbeam through the shutter. Hellison catches his breath. Hellison closes his eyes. Hellison sits in the guest bedroom until he hears his wife come home. It is dark. Hellison reaches for the Wind Catalog. Hellison removes his wallet from his pocket and his MasterCard from his wallet and reaches for the telephone.

Once upon a time there was a television commercial for shampoo which began with a beautiful young lady telling us how she used the product and told two friends and they told two friends and they told two friends and by the end of the commercial the screen fills with a mosaic of the beautiful young lady repeated over and over and over and this is what happens in terms of the Wind Catalog once Hellison described as best he could to his friends what he felt when he opened #35.

Did it make you sad?

Not at all.

Not even a little sad.

Perhaps afterwards.

Well that's not good.

Only a little sad.

Sadness is never good except when it is good.

The sadness was minimal.

Then it was nostalgia you felt.

I wouldn't say that exactly.

Then say something exactly.

I felt like I was living in the moment.

Your moment.

It might have been someone else's moment.

But a moment that reminded you of one of your own moments.

There was no remembering, there was living.

And what did you do with the empty canister? Recycled it.

They turned to their copies of the Wind Catalog and bought. Currents. Breezes. Chinooks. Drafts. Gales. Gusts. Mistrals. Puffs. Tempests. Typhoons. Cyclones. Waftings. Whisks. Zephyrs. Breaths.

Savings accounts were depleted. Canisters large and small overflowed the recycling bins. They who had never been to Nebraska bought Nebraska wind. They who had never been to Paris bought Paris wind. They who had never been on a motorcycle bought wind rushing past a motorcyclist. They put their canisters in the corners of their rooms and opened the lids and closed their eyes and lived in their moments and emerged from their rooms with new realizations painted on their amazed faces. They became tolerant of small children. They became seductive to long-endured spouses. They read every section of the newspaper. They drank more expensive wine. They walked. They talked. They wondered.

The wonder, as you are well aware, never ends. A few of them wondered where it was all coming from and tracked the Classic Wind Consortium to a cinderblock building in the Ozarks. They found no one on the premises. The door was open. They walked inside. They discovered thirty thousand square feet of darkness.

We do not care where it comes from or who fills the canisters or if the canisters are actually filled. We do not care. We do not care how they collect what they collect or by what method they collect what they collect or whose idea it was in the first place. We do not give a damn. We do not give a damn who decides that a first toboggan ride in a forest preserve in Iowa circa 1974 (#197) is worth sixty bucks or a post-fireworks backyard circa 1946 (#355) is worth seventy-five or a World Series 7th inning stretch after a light rain circa 1968 (#54a-b-c) is worth three hundred we do not care we do not care we want it we want this we want this always.

They bought and they bought and they wanted more and they waited for the third edition of the Wind Catalog and while they waited they tried new things and ordered new orders and experienced what they never thought they would experience or would like to experience and they wondered. They wondered who was collecting now. They wondered if the unseen and unknown entrepreneurs who had been collecting for the past two hundred years were still collecting, were passing on their knowledge to their mysterious inheritors. They felt that someday in the future they would possibly like to shell out for a canister full of a particularly nice day they were experiencing, or an exciting time, or a romantic time, or a trying time, or an ordinary time. They wondered if someone was collecting all or as much as they could of the unseen, busy, rushing atmosphere around them, the wind that comes the wind that goes the wind that is remembering. They wonder and they wait for the next Wind Catalog.

We are still waiting.

A Brief Survey of
Faulty Contraception

Kilff knew they didn't like him, but he would change all that. Oh yes, he thought, they don't like me now, but they're going to love me. There's no crowd like a tough crowd.

Twenty minutes later, when he had finished, they were on their feet, smiling, giving him a hearty hand. Their remarks afterwards were the same as the remarks he always heard after similar luncheons: "You're a funny guy," and "That was great," and "Best ever," and "We should have you again next year." He said his thank you's, looked around for the guy who would hand him his check (always in a business envelope with a cellophane window), and left, pausing long enough on the sidewalk to smoke a cigarette and perhaps catch a few more jolly words of praise from early leavers.

They hadn't listened, not really. Oh, they had heard this and that, but they hadn't truly listened to a thing he had said. It wasn't that they had been polite about the topic; these kinds of people who were every kind of people weren't polite about such thing. It was that Kilff brought them confidence and humor and flair. He didn't rely on jokes, nor did he know any. He could be funny merely by the way he expressed himself, or so he had been told more than once by people who didn't have a vested interest in his future. He had charm. He was open. He could name his price.

He could also talk up the women, if he was addressing a mixed crowd. He had yet to break into the solely female circuit, but he knew he would, eventually. He survived on word-of-mouth, and for the past year the words from the mouths had been consistently laudatory. He had come to a point where if he wasn't exactly turning down every engagement he was offered, he was turning down at least one every three months or so. As for the women, when they were there he lingered longer afterwards and let the check-bearer find him. One these occasions, he would allow the conversations to bleed into the bar of the banquet hall or down the block to some corner watering hole with a single television perched in a high corner. The women would be free and open and serious with him. He would take out his wallet.

"Hard to believe he'd be ten years old if he were still with us," he'd say, showing them a photograph of one of his nephews. "Yes, ten years old Tuesday. My son. My only child. He ... it's ... well, I shouldn't have brought it up." He could not manage tears, he could only get his eyes to go a little watery, but tears were inadvisable anyway. Tears would be going overboard, and people recoil from tears coming out of a man. The holding back of tears, however, usually got the ladies back to his apartment or hotel room if his engagement was out of town.

To be fair, he always wanted to know what people wanted him to talk about. At first, he spent a great deal of time getting to know his audience before he met his audience, and after his fifth or sixth success he realized all audiences were the same whether the miasma of the luncheon or dinner or banquet or awards show was theater, shoe sales, medicine, transportation, business, real estate, tax laws, agriculture, firearms, gaming, Buddhism, fetishes, unwed mothers, or unwed fathers. He was an entertainment, nothing else. A spellbinder. He could be as unprepared as he liked and they would still laugh, applaud, become misty-eyed—anything he wanted. He could blather on and on about anything that came into his head, and did. They listened but they didn't. He gave a lecture entitled "Ancient Methodologies for Royal Vasectomies" to a group of art historians and was lionized. He made a speech called "An Abridged History of Mouth Cankers" to a group of abstemious Rotarians and was cheered. His house specialty, "A Brief Survey of Faulty Contraception," to which he found himself returning with increasing frequency, had nearly made him legendary. He never made notes or wrote out his texts. A jangle of words or contrary phrases would come to him and he would pencil them down on an index card, tuck it into his pocket, and launch himself into whatever he was going to say for however long he was required to say it. In some ways and for different reasons he was more amazed at his presentations than anyone else.

Otherwise, he was nothing. He shopped with a plastic basket slung around one arm rather than a shopping cart because his needs were few and his tastes never varied. He maintained his income by hanging onto the same job he had had for twenty-two years, a job that required him to sit under frosted fluorescents in a corner of a sizeable room shared with two other people whom he never saw except when he left the room to use the bathroom or go to lunch because the three of them were separated by pockmarked beige dividers. He drove to and from his office in a nondescript vehicle painted nickel silver and occasionally went for a walk around his small suburb. He liked to sit and read. He could actually envision himself sitting and reading by the light of a single lamp with a water glass half-filled with cheap cream sherry on the table next to him while bland chamber music dribbled from his stereo. He could live it and see it at the same time; in fact, everything he did he could see and live simultaneously and he wondered why that was. He rarely remembered anything about anything he read, but he enjoyed reading so that's what he did when he wasn't shopping or walking or working or driving or having sex with some woman he had charmed after one of his engagements.

"How'd you get started doing this?" one had asked after sex. He honestly didn't know, but told her, "I was at this big event and the guest speaker hadn't shown up, so I was cajoled into stepping in and I was a big hit. I was nervous as all hell, but I'm a courageous person, I knocked back what was left of my drink and went up to the podium with a smile and a head held high." He couldn't understand why he couldn't remember the circumstances of his initiation as a host/master of ceremonies/lecturer/guest speaker. He had no reason to block out the memory, and his first time wasn't exactly a long time ago, yet he couldn't for the life of him recall when, where, or why he had embarked on his new career and, unlike the rest of his life, he couldn't envision himself doing it while he was doing it. Another young lady, in another hotel room, had said, "You must have started somewhere," and he had lied and said, "I was staying at some big hotel downtown and about to check out when I saw a bride sobbing in the lobby because the best man had passed out drunk and he was supposed to give this great talk but he had ruined everything, so I told her she could introduce me as her something-or-other and I'd make everything okay, so she did and I did, and there was this guy there who said to me afterwards he'd like me to come speak to his board and I did and things just picked up from there."

He could give anybody any answer, and as long as he gave it without hesitation he was believed and it never bothered him.

What had bothered him for a little while was that whatever good looks he had as a young man had become blanched and softened by the time he was thirty-five. His hair hadn't gone gray but its color had certainly exhausted itself. His body had yet to run to fat, but it had become pillowish. He saw himself seeing himself, looking at himself, sometimes for minutes, in mirrors and reflective surfaces. He found a pencil and wrote "The Excremental Habits of Gangrenous Carpenters" on an index card and slid it into the pocket of his gray sport coat. He wrote "Born into Penury and Disgrace: The Life of Wilella J. Southcott" on another and slid it into the pocket of his tan sport coat. He wrote "Reflectories" on another and slid it into his blue sport coat. He knew not who Wilella J. Southcott was, because the name had only come to him then. He knew not what a reflectory was, because the word had only just then flashed through his brain. He knew not if carpenters, when they become gangrenous, have any sort of habits, excremental or otherwise. He would find out when he spoke.

Eventually, he left his office job and sat around waiting for further speaking engagements, which began to fill his weeks and weekends. He spent money on another three sport coats and even purchased formal wear, which he had tailored, a service that made him feel like Someone. He stopped going to the grocery store every week because he was being fed sumptuous breakfasts, extravagant luncheons, and outrageous dinners. On one particular Sunday he spoke at all three mealtimes and made himself sick. He began to become queasy at the mere mention of word "buffet." He began to manage his calendar better after that, and while he didn't think he was leading "the good life," he did see himself leading something while he was leading it.

He warmed to the outrageous topics that he pulled from his pockets. His disquisition on secret insemination cults almost surpassed the popularity of his faulty contraception survey. People shook his hand, slapped his back. Red faces, shiny faces, mirth and earnestness. "I wish you'd work for me," some often said. "What a communicator," some others often said. He continued to trot out a string of fictional dead wives, dead children, and dead pets to the ladies as he led them to motel boudoirs.

"That was total bullshit," a woman said to him one night. "Bravo."

Kilff didn't know how to respond to her. She seemed benign enough. He sensed no challenge. He looked for a nametag and, finding none, asked the woman her name.

"I'll tell you my name is Nicki," she said. "That good enough?"

"I suppose it'll have to be," he said. "Now as for my talk being total bullshit..."

"Oh, you don't have to defend yourself to me. I'm not judging. I just want you to know that someone noticed."

"I haven't admitted..."

"Listen, it's okay. You're very engaging and funny, but I noticed."

"What did you notice?"

"Your disdain for us."

"Not true. I have no disdain; I am full of dain, in fact, and..."

"Look, I said I'm not judging you, nor am I calling you out. You're a pro. And you managed to somehow make them all think your blather had something to do with them, although for the life of me I couldn't figure out what exactly faulty contraception had to do with the projected spatula production for the upcoming fiscal year."

"Is that what you people do? Make spatulas?"

"Among other things. Didn't you know? Well, of course you didn't know. You're here for the paycheck and the free eats, and I'm totally down with that. Again—all I'm doing is complimenting you on your gimmick but also letting you know that I know how you operate and therefore wasn't taken in."

Kilff felt his ears redden and took a quick glance around the reception hall for someone, anyone. What could he say to this woman who admitted she had given him a false name?

"What can I say to you?" he said. "And why the false name?"

"You can't say anything to me. Well, you can say anything you like to me; what I meant was there's no need for you to say anything to me. I don't need an explanation and I'm not criticizing you. Or condemning you."

"Then what do you want?"

"To tell you we're not all alike."

"I never said you were."

"That every now and then you're going to run into someone who totally sees your spiel for what it is and why it sells. That's all."

She walked away. He followed her.

"This isn't a racket," he said to her. "It's not what you think."

"Okay."

"Wait. I mean it. That's not a line I'm handing you. I'm not... I don't come up with this stuff because I think you're all vacuous sheep who... I'm being honest here, I'm not taking advantage of..." He fished his wallet out of his coat and began digging for photographs. "Listen, I've been kind of mixed up recently, what with the untimely passing of my son..."

She smiled. "Oh, come on," she said. "Your son? Really?"

He produced a photo of his sister. "My wife?"

She rolled her eyes. "Yeah, right," she said. "Look, don't press your luck. I'm not going to put anybody wise to the reality of your routine, so you don't have to play the dead loved one card to get my sympathy or whatever it is you want me to show that I'm not showing." She pointed to the photos. "You don't keep family photos folded up with your cash. Now let's just leave it at that. You have a terrific personality when you're up behind a podium and it's fascinating to see you in action, to try to figure out how your mind is coming up with that drivel and why you've chosen to wing it like that in the first place, but don't lower yourself to lying."

He went to put the photos back in his wallet but changed his mind and shoved them into his coat pocket. "Maybe you and I got off on the wrong foot..."

"A survey of faulty contraception," she said, the smug smile still on her face. "Brilliant. Is that always your gimmick or do you mix it up with other crap? I'm guessing you mix it up. I sort of wish I could see you at other events. I could be your groupie."

He thought for a moment about handing her a come-on about the hotness and willingness of groupies and endorsing her desire for such a scenario, but then thought better of it and said, "What's your real name?"

"I'll tell you my real name is Adriana," she said, then turned and headed towards the exit.

"That doesn't mean Adriana is your real name!" he said, and she was gone.

Kilff spent the next few weeks trying to see himself doing his speaking engagements, just as he saw himself in his apartment sitting and reading and listening to music or in his car or in his office, but he still couldn't manage it. He stood up at every luncheon table, mounted every dais, and spoke into every microphone just as he always had, each time pulling a card from his pocket and reacting to the words he saw. He tried to understand why he had written the words he had written and their connection to himself. Was "reflectory" a combination of reflection and rectory in his mind and, if so, what had those two things to do with him? Had he become overly sensitive to the blurry man he saw in the mirror? Had he ever been to a rectory? What had gangrene and excrement to do with his life? Was he somehow subconsciously attracted to the putrid and disgusting? No. And what of carpentry? He'd never built anything in his life, not even a house of playing cards. Was he a product of faulty contraception?

And all the while he saw Nicki/Adriana walking away from him.

There were more luncheons, banquets, ceremonies. There were more words, falsehoods. There was more applause. But after every round of applause, he waited for Nicki/Adriana to approach him again, perhaps attach herself to him and try to persuade him to change his spiel, the one thing she hadn't tried to do when he met her. It didn't happen, and after a while he stopped hauling his wallet out, stopped showing the photographs of the son and wife he never had, stopped trying to see himself doing things that he was doing.

"There is a moment," he would tell this or that woman, "that feels like a short spasm of eternity between being introduced and opening my mouth when it feels like everyone is against me, hating me, waiting for me to fail, to be lousy; a moment when I hear them thinking *too short, too fat, too pale, too bald, too soft, too smarmy, too boring, too creepy* and on and on and on and on. Tidal waves of negativity. I feel it.

"It's my job to convince you, however, that I know what I'm doing, that you are safe in my hands, that what I say is true not because of what I'm saying but the manner in which I'm saying it. The most outrageous statements become bromides; the most offensive topics become Sunday school chat. It's not that I believe what I'm saying but that I believe I can make you believe I believe what I'm saying." At this point, he would leave his drink unfinished and cast a glance over the hundreds of people still milling about, drinking, smiling, talking, seeking, and meeting. "Ask me what will happen if one day I actually believe what I'm saying."

He is always asked. He never answers.

Blue Tangle

My solution to the whole thing is have Freckert leave town, begin anew somewhere else, screw up the lives of others unknown to us, and I tell him so, I tell him, "Bladensburg is nice," and he asks me where that is, and I tell him, "Maryland, of course."

"It's that 'of course' that infuriates me," he says. "Not everybody knows as much as you do. You don't have to rub our stupidity in our faces." Meanwhile, Darla is leaving him another message on his voicemail. I don't have to hear it to know it. I know it because Freckert's phone keeps chiming. "How can you stand it?" I ask, and he says, "I tune it out."

Which is what he did to Hafe, and Hafe didn't like it, or at least I assume Hafe didn't like it because he stopped coming to me about it. I am not Freckert's keeper. I am many things to Freckert, and keeper is definitely not one of them. Well, all right, in a small way I am indeed Freckert's keeper, perhaps you could say I am the keeper of a selection of Freckert's secrets, which is to say a selection of things Freckert wants to keep secret but, in actuality, is merely a slew of things he thinks are secret that the rest of us know. He says he can't help himself. Who can? I ask.

I coffee with Serena.

"I don't know how he got there, but he got there," she says. "Couch to my bed, suddenly, and me not remembering the transition. Not immediately going at it once in the bed, but more like on the bed for a long time, talking about something. Spooning, if you want to call it that. It was more like a slow grinding, almost imperceptible, the way two turtles would do it if turtles did that sort of thing."

"And what led to it?" I ask.

"He was frustrated about Hafe," she says.

"Was he specific?"

"Oh, yes and no. There was so much. Not enough this, not ready to do that, really nice this, occasional that. You know."

"I've heard. Some things."

"If anyone would know, it would be you."

"I wonder why everyone thinks that."

"Because you and he were you and he. And maybe still are."

"But he was on the bed with you."

"Yes."

I ask Freckert to explain Serena.

"I can't," he says.

"And Darla?" I ask. "Still leaving messages?"

"Yes, and carving her feet."

"Carving her feet?"

"Nothing serious. Superficial wounds. Makes it difficult for her to walk in sandals."

"And all over you?"

"So she says. I think she's been doing it for a good long while, however. I think it's her thing. An attention-getter."

"If she wanted attention, she wouldn't be cutting the soles of her feet," I say. "Who sees the soles?"

"A visitor, if she sits cross-legged on her bed while smoking."

"And she does that often?"

"Which?"

"Sit cross-legged on the bed. I already know she smokes like a coal refinery."

"Oh. Yes. Well, she can't sit anywhere else in that pit of hers. Crap everywhere. You have to sit on the floor, if you can find a patch of uncluttered floor. And then you're eye-level to those cut-up feet of hers."

"Yes. Yes, I know."

"Oh? What's your experience with her?"

"To avoid the view of the feet, I sat on the bed."

"With her."

"Yes."

"And?"

"The same fate as you."

"I see. It's all a trap."

"Not a trap. A stage_managing."

I omelet with Hafe. He says little. He has said all he wants to say about Freckert. I decipher his expressions. The first is vague. The second is bunched. The third is furrowed. I ask him why he is depressed then sad then angry. He wants to know how I know he was all those things. I don't give away my secrets. I recommend Darla to him. He goes. I realize my mistake; I should have recommended him to Serena. I don't go after him.

"I've looked into Bladensburg," says Freckert. "It's not for me."

"If not Bladensburg," I say, "then anywhere will do. Anywhere not near."

"How far is not near?"

"A goodly distance."

"Such as?"

"Anything drivable in one afternoon."

"I'm not at fault, you know."

"I know."

And I am not lying to him when I tell him that I know he is not at fault. He isn't. What he is is the hub. I don't tell him he's the hub and therefore construed as the fault. I know there are more involved than Darla and Serena and Hafe. There are many more, overlapping. It's hard to tell who's the latest, who's the first. Perhaps there is no first. I ask him.

"There's always a first," he says. "I just don't recall their names." I'm surprised by the plurality, but not really. I ask. "Two cousins," he says. "Two cousins on a visit from an arid state once known for agriculture."

"Cousins? Of yours?" I ask.

"Yes."

"But you can't remember their names?"

"Distant cousins. Once met, never seen again. Back to their turnips and farm equipment and endless fields of dusty gray-yellow. One boy, one girl, both my age or thereabouts, both interested in me at the same time, the same hour, the same bedroom, the mouths of two related strangers on my neck. I don't want to revisit the memory."

I comfort Serena. When finished, she thanks me for the four-minute orgasm; hers, not mine. I tell her I find that difficult to believe. She asks me to take her word for it. I tell her I don't need bolstering. She sobs.

"Because Hafe was just here two nights ago," she says.

"Why was he here?"

"He said he was here by accident."

"And you made the most of it?"

"One minute we were on the couch, the next we were in here, on the bed."

"I thought that was what happened with Freckert?"

"It was."

"And the same with Hafe?"

"Sort of. In Hafe's instance, I'm more aware of the transitions. I definitely engineered Hafe into this bed."

"Amazing."

"Well, what could I do? He said he came to see me by accident, and I decided to make the most of the accident."

I pizza with Hafe and suggest he and I make an attempt at consoling Darla since he hadn't been able to act upon my original recommendation to him. We visit Darla and make the suggestion.

She will have none of it.

Freckert's wife visits. We are all surprised.

"She ran off with Georgia," Freckert tells me.

"When was this?" I ask. We are on a balcony.

"Oh, before."

"Before what?"

"Before now, obviously."

"I meant before whom."

"Before Dundinger."

"Dundinger?"

"You don't know him."

"And did all this happen because Georgia knew about Dundinger?"

"I met Dundinger through Georgia."

"So Georgia was the cause of Dundinger?"

"Hardly. Georgia has nothing to do with Dundinger."

"Aside from the introduction."

"Exactly."

"And where is Dundinger now?"

"Ask Serena."

I ask Serena. She doesn't remember. She asks me to describe him. I can't because he wasn't described to me by Freckert. I tell her about Georgia. She says, "I often wondered." I'm not sure what she's often wondered about, and she doesn't tell me when I ask.

I tell Hafe about Dundinger. He isn't surprised.

"You knew of Dundinger?" I ask.

"Dundinger and I look very much alike," he says.

I give up on Dundinger, who is obviously somewhere else or never existed. Darla summons me. I visit her, insisting we go for a walk. She minces along, her feet healing. She knows I know about her foot situation but won't give me the satisfaction of knowing I know about her foot situation, nor does she wish to trade on her discomfort. I take it easy on her and we stop to rest two blocks from her apartment building in a cement playground a few yards from the lake.

"We could have been something," she says.

"You and Freckert?" I ask.

"You and me."

"When?"

"When you came by with Hafe."

"You don't like Hafe?"

"He's decent enough."

"Then you're referring to you and me from before."

"Yes. Stupid, right?"

"Not stupid. Unfortunate."

"Send him back."

"Freckert?"

"No, Hafe."

"I don't know if he'll come."

"Send him with Serena."

I send Hafe and Serena to Darla and tell Freckert things might be sorting themselves out. He tells me he doesn't care, he's moving to Maryland.

"Bladensburg?" I ask.

"No, but nearby. I don't want anyone to know."

"Then you shouldn't have told me."

"Rats."

We watch boats on the water, birds swooping.

"I suppose that since you know you'd better come with me," he says.

"And what of Georgia?"

"What's Georgia got to do with it?"

"She's your wife."

"No. Inez is my wife."

I think back as hard as I can. Of course. Freckert's wife, when she appeared, was simply Freckert's wife, her name never mentioned. Georgia is the woman with whom she ran off, and suddenly my heads hurts.

"What's the matter?" Freckert asks.

"Nothing," I say. "I hope you find Maryland to your liking."

"It's the only way out of this," he says, arms folded, eyes on the water. "Staying here where all of you can get at me isn't going to solve anything."

"You're not at fault."

"I'm the hub."

"All of us are the hub." The sun is setting behind us, and I turn away from the endless water to the jagged wall of buildings. "Hafe has now got you, Serena, Darla...and possibly me. No, wait—not me. Almost me. Darla, in turn, has me, you, Hafe, Serena, and who knows who else."

"And Hafe has Dundinger," he says. "Had."

"Really?"

"I'm pretty sure."

"And your wife? Inez?"

"I'm not sure who she'll do."

"You mean what she'll do."

"Yes to both."

There is no cold colder than a sunset shadow on the back of one's neck. When I stop thinking about everything, I notice Freckert walking away. Yes, I think. That is the easiest untanglement, and also the most difficult. Cut loose and leave the knot knotted.

I juice with Georgia.

Certain Elements Combined

They are training for something. We are aware of this. There are nine of them we know and a few more whom we do not clearly know. We listen to everything they say when they are near the things we use to listen to them. We can see them together and apart. There are many of us as well. There are perhaps more of us than them and that is a small comfort.

Osteraas is the youngest of them. He is sixteen. He is big for sixteen but not fat. He frightens most of us because he is the youngest and the most passionate even though we are aware his passion is most likely imitative. He is in love with a girl named Ima. She lives in the village.

We should not be observing them. We should be infiltrating them. One of us should be infiltrating them. This is in some ways impossible now. So we are telling Ima all she needs to know about Osteraas and them and we are encouraging her to love Osteraas. Ima does not want trouble with anyone. Not with us and not with them. And anyway she is in love with Osteraas only not as much as he is with her and that is all fine and dandy. We are grateful she is so young.

All of them are big on gun rights and wary of Washington. Osteraas never concluded this for himself because he is the youngest and because he was born into it. He was born hearing it. He has grown up to be big for his age and most frightening while hearing all of it. That's him there, carrying his Level 1 gear like it's as light as an egg sandwich.

Osteraas shows Ima everything on their first date. The FRS radio. The four magazines of thirty rounds each for the rifle. The compass. The military-style knife. The 9mm sidearm. The two magazines for the sidearm. Ima gives him something to wear. It is her necklace. The necklace has a gold-plated heart-shaped locket depending from it. There is nothing in the locket. Osteraas wears it. At night he sprawls on his bed and thinks something holy has happened.

The eldest one of the group does all of the talking which is mostly the same things over and over again said the same way or nearly the same way. We are hearing him again now and it's all many of us can do to keep from saying his words along with him:

If we were free in this nation we would not need a birth certificate or a driver's license or a building permit. We would not need a social security number to get a job.

Osteraas is in the woods with Ima. He is showing her something. He is showing her how to make a bow drill fire. He is telling her only two percent of the population can make a bow drill fire. Ima asks him if he is wearing the locket. He puts his hand on his chest.

We are doing and have been doing for some time a great deal of sitting. Much of this sitting involves a great deal of listening. A great deal of this listening is listening to nothing or more accurately listening to silence. Listening to silence is different from listening to nothing. Carvel taught this to me early on. Carvel said to me and the others on several occasions *Listening to nothing is impossible unless you are in a vacuum or in outer space. Listening to silence is listening to everything that can be heard when there is nothing being said.* We are always doing a great deal of listening to everything that can be heard when there is no talking. We have learned to listen to textures. We are hearing the rapid paddy of someone using a handheld communication device. We are hearing an overlap of something small and hard being freed from a cellophane wrapper. We are hearing another overlap of the scrubby process of a bag being opened and closed followed by the mushy crinkle of a plastic bag and unmistakeableness of coins. Carvel is so used to the sounds of everything that he can call off nickel or dime or quarter as he hears them. This is very amusing for a little while. Gollenweiser has taken to showing off as she can differentiate coughs and clearings and phlegm. She calls out bronchitis or cold or congestion or allergy or smoker as she hears them. Her favorite is Too Much Nasal Hair. None of us are able to challenge her ears. We have never been able to challenge Carvel's ears. They have their specialties and it is all very entertaining for a little while. We listen and we nod. We hear something we cannot identify. We want to hear it again.

Osteraas has his hand up Ima's shirt and we are all remembering what it was like to be young and intense. We think Osteraas is too young to be so young and intense. He has failed to teach Ima how to make a bow drill fire even though he has been a thorough and patient teacher for one so young and intense. We watch Ima practicing the bow drill fire on her own when no one is looking. She cannot do it. She gives up and walks away and then comes back to it which is a new kind of persistence to us.

Osteraas is telling her he is not a racist and not paranoid. He is telling her without telling her he is not a misconception. Ima takes off her shirt.

We are listening to the leader never call their militia a militia. He is always saying *defensive organization*.

Some of us are doing and have been doing a great deal of watching. The watching some of us are doing occurs separately from the listening some of us others are doing. Somewhere the two things are being wed. Gollenweiser continues to not understand why one is separate from the other. Carvel tells her there is a place where it all comes together to be seen by someone or a group of someones. In some ways at many times the listeners are envying the watchers and the same is true for the watchers envying the listeners at many times.

We are listening a great deal to anger. We are hearing anger over changing demographics in the country and anger over soaring public debt and anger over a troubled economy and the anger over the perception that the President's initiatives are socialist or fascist or sometimes both. Gollenweiser told me yesterday she wants to be a watcher. Carvel heard what she said and told her she is fine where she is and how she is a damn fine listener. Someone coughs. Gollenweiser says *Went down wrong pipe* without even thinking about it. We have never met the watchers but someday when this is all over perhaps someone will throw a party for all of us and then we can know who we are.

The eldest of the militia is talking again:

The people of this country and some people around the world are waiting just waiting for a certain kind of individual I mean individuals like the ones you see here because we're supposed to be down there making the decision to go to war against the evil and greedy new world order that is now in existence.

Osteraas is so young at sixteen his voice cracks when he is excited. We made fun of this at first but do not make fun of it anymore. He says nothing when he is in the presence of the leader and he is with the leader moderately often. He speaks when he is spoken to and the leader never speaks to him only speaks at him.

None of us can get a clear picture or complete picture of Osteraas or the leader or anyone and Carvel tells us not to worry because Someone is.

We are listening to Ima show Osteraas how to have sex with her and we are making nervous jokes about everything we hear but we are in reality anticipatory and eager and interested in this moment between them. We can only imagine what the watchers are seeing. We wonder if the watchers need the sounds to understand. Of course they don't. And we don't need to see. Many things we have to look at and listen to carefully but not this. There is an overlap of dead leaves.

Gollenweiser calls off sick one day because of a cold. She returns the next day and doesn't say anything about anything.

We are collectively seeing and hearing now how all of them are always at Level 10. They are not doing civil ambushes. They are doing military ambushes. They are practicing concealment. They are doing fire team movements.

Someone late in the game says we have been stupid because we could be getting everything at all times. We ask how. Someone says *The locket.* We are asking Ima if she can get the locket back and when she asks why we say because we want to put something in it. Ima says she doesn't know if she can or even if she wants to.

And because of this we are recalling what it was like to be young and intense but we are not recalling when this youth and intensity died within us. We begin to worry because it is alarming to us now to realize we did not know it died within us at the time it died within us. We want that locket back so we can put something in it so we can hear everything clearly at all times because it lives around Osteraas's neck until Gollenweiser says *All we'd hear is his heartbeat.*

There is a day when plans are being discussed and everything is being made clear for them and likewise to the unseen us. We end what we are doing because beyond the listeners and the watchers there are some of us who will be doing the ending of them because that is their specialty. We understand this in them and in us and it is anyone's guess if Osteraas will come out of it alive although there is no reason to think otherwise except for the fact that there is always a reason to think otherwise because anything could happen. We have all we need for now and all we need to prevent anything further from happening and so we look as long as we can and listen as long as we can. Just a little longer. Anticipating the ending. Because Ima has finally figured out how to make a bow drill fire and Osteraas is very much more in love with her because of this and for other reasons and because all we can see and hear is a spark, a spark that will lead to a fire.

Score

Jessica normally lets everything go to voicemail, but she notices the caller's 212 area code. She answers. It's Richard. He says, "It's been a long time, sorry about that, things have been crazy-busy, and this is sudden, I know, but I'm wondering if, hoping you could do me a solid."

"Sure, if I can."

"Great. Listen, I'm assistant conductor on *Works for Beginners...*"

"That's great."

"Yeah, and you know what that means, Keyboard One, and I have to get out of town like tonight and I'm looking for somebody to take over, and I figured, hey, it's Chicago and who do I know, who'd be the best. You. What do you say?"

"I say no problem."

"Really?"

"Who's the musical director?"

"Kay Marfitt."

"No shit. I gave her her first job, you know. Back in the day. One of my own musicals, needed a second keyboardist, she called in or something, I hired her. Or rather Natalie Glyman did, she was the musical director on *Union Street*, remember her? I think she's running a youth musicals program somewhere in Idaho now."

"Sure, Natalie. So, you're in?"

"As long Kay's fine with it. I don't think Kay likes me."

"She loves you. Why do you think she doesn't like you?"

"I never hear from her."

"Well, she never responds to anything, she's everywhere these days. Don't take it personally."

"Does she know you were going to ask me?"

"She knows, I mentioned it to her, she said ,'Oh, Jessica!' like she was excited, and why not?"

"How'd you get around the contractor?"

"Skip's old and doesn't care—do you know Skip? Skip Lutter?"

"Um…"

"Well, he's fine with it, said, 'If you're going to vouch for her, fine, bring her in.' He doesn't want any hassles, we have enough trouble getting him to stay awake between cues."

"How old is this guy?"

"He's like a hundred and twelve, he goes way back, says he played the pit of *The Music Man*, like its original run for Christ's sake."

"And he's playing *Works for Beginners?*"

"He's tripling reeds, I guess he's the only guy alive can still play a bass sax."

"There's a bass sax in the pit?"

"This thing's scored up the wazoo, almost twenty-five pieces, they've got the money, you wouldn't believe it. Strings and everything. Hey, there's an Asian dude playing first violin, you'll love him, if I know you, unless all that's changed, I don't know, none of my business, but if memory serves…"

"I don't know, a lot can change in however long it's been, like fifteen years."

"Anyway, if it hasn't, icing on the cake, right? Like 'em young?"

"Um..."

"Anyway, Skip said as long as you've got your union card..."

"Oh, I have it, I have it. Dues all paid up and everything."

"I figured you did, I got your number out of the federation directory. That was his only worry, so great, great. So can you come over to the Cadillac tomorrow about nine? In the morning?"

"Yeah, sure, I got nothing—I mean, I'll have to rearrange some things, but nothing I can't cancel or shove around. But listen, what's the story here? What's the pay?"

"Oh yeah, the pay, right? Here I am running off at the mouth trying to get you hooked into this and I'm leaving out the gravy. The pay. Well, you'd just be getting Keyboard One, a little over scale, no doubling or anything, gone are the days of the live celesta, huh? So only the keyboard..."

"What kind? Upright? Synth?"

"Synth? That's so early 90's. You're kidding, right? No, digital. No way can we fit a real piano down there, not with all the strings we got."

"Sure, sure."

"It's all programmed, if that's what you're worried about."

"No, I'm good, I'm not worried. It's all good, all good. I'm still just a little...I mean, I haven't heard from you in such a long time, and now..."

"Yeah, horrible, my fault, totally. Listen, now I hope you won't be offended, it's nothing personal, but before you get confused about it or say something and step on somebody's toes, we're only paying you, I mean they're only hiring you for Keyboard One, you won't be assuming the role of assistant conductor, that'll still be me."

"Sure, sure. No, I get it. It didn't even occur to me to ask about that, I figured Keyboard One and that's it. Is everything okay?"

"Sure."

"Well, you said you had to get out of town like pronto, so I'm wondering, although it's none of my business, you sound kind of rushed, I'm just wondering if everything's okay."

"Yeah, everything's fine. Well, I hope everything's fine. I got a call this morning, Lina got hit between 72nd and 73rd, I don't know what she was doing way down there."

"Lina?"

"My wife. Didn't you know we got married?"

"You mean Lina Rosenthal?"

"The very same."

"Oh my God. Seriously? You married Lina?"

"Yeah, Jesus, I guess it has been a long time, wow, how would you know? You left New York, I just assumed you still know what's going on with everybody, you know? Yeah, Lina and me, eight years come July."

"Well. Well well well. Congratulations, eight million years later. But you said she got hit?"

"Jogging, yeah. I'm a wreck. I mean, they told me she's fine, she'll live, but I've got to be there, right?"

"Definitely. Oh yes, definitely."

"So I'm on the first plane out of here, the first one I could get on, flying out of O'Hare in . . . yikes, like five hours."

"Poor Lina. Oh, I hope everything's okay!"

"Yeah, thanks. Fingers crossed. Anyway, so you see why you're not getting assistant conductor, I'm hoping I'll be back soon, I just don't think I'm going to be around for first preview or all of next week, and besides, a sub is a sub, I'm not there one day it's a catastrophe, and the kid playing Keyboard Two, well, he's a smart kid, talented, we're doing him a favor, or we're doing somebody a favor, probably Larriman, have you ever met him?"

"Met who? The kid playing the other keyboard part or Larriman?"

"Larriman."

"Oh, so it's a Larriman score."

"Yeah, didn't you know?"

"I only know the show's doing its out-of-town tryout here; I wasn't really paying attention to who wrote it."

"Is it a problem?"

"No, no, piece of cake. I'll limber up. Hey, I still use the Czerny you gave me, remember?"

"Get out. You do?"

"Well, when I mean I still use it, I mean I have it handy. It's in the piano bench, you know, prime location, it's right there, I'm sitting on it all the time, ha ha. But it's not like I use it in the sense that I still have to use it, I mean it's good for a brush up now and then, you know, something to keep the fingers nimble and the mind keen, as Dr. Schott used to say."

"Now there's a name! I wonder how he's doing? Still grinding away, huh?"

"No, I heard he died. Couple of years ago. He was sick for a long time."

"Well, he never looked healthy back in the day. Yellow, you know, and like his skin was made of that, um, what's that dough you use to make strudel?"

"Filo."

"Right. So, hey. Look. You're cool with this? Keyboard One, tomorrow, nine?"

"I'm cool. Anyway I could look at the score beforehand?"

"Gosh, no. I mean, the only way we could do that is if I got it to you somehow, but I don't know how that's going to happen what with me flying out of here in the next couple hours. I could take a cab, but you're ... where are you, out in the suburbs or something?"

"I'm in Grossdale, maybe a twenty, twenty-five minute drive from the Loop."

"God, the boonies! What the hell are you doing way out there?"

"Well ..."

"So no doubt you've got a car."

"Yes, I have a car ..."

"Wow, you've really like settled down and everything."

"Well, I wouldn't say settled down, exactly ..."

"But anyway, the score. Yeah. Even if I could bring it out to you or you came up here to the hotel, which you haven't time for, really, even if you left like five minutes ago, I've still got to make a couple more calls, pack, get my ass out to O'Hare, even if all that could happen I haven't got the thing on me, the librarian's got it ..."

"The librarian?"

"That's our nickname for Yunisho, he used to work with the Pittsburgh Symphony, he's that good, he was third chair or something and their score librarian, and man, I'm telling you, you're going to flip for him, and he's very flirty ..."

"Listen, my tastes, I mean my preferences, you know, have sort of changed over the years, I mean people change, you know, I'm not just crazy for Asian guys anymore ..."

"That's good, that's fine, I didn't mean to get you upset..."

"I'm not upset, but—what? Am I only known, am I only remembered for one thing?"

"No, not at all. That's not what I'm saying. Forget about Yunisho, forget I said anything. The point is nobody can get you the music until tomorrow, that's why we'd like you to come in at nine, just so you can get the lay of the land, so to speak, before everybody gets going."

"Gets going with what?"

"First preview."

"Tomorrow?"

"It's not until eight, don't worry, you'll have all day to practice, if you need it."

"You didn't tell me tomorrow's the first preview! With an audience and everything?"

"That's the plan."

"Richard..."

"Hey, if anyone can do it, it's you. Total faith in you. Best sight reader ever, even better than Kay, although don't tell her I said that, not that she has to do much sight reading anymore, I mean the last time she had to touch a piano was maybe ten years ago. But you, the best! Everybody knew that, they know that. So don't worry. You know Larriman's style, this show's just like his others, maybe a little mellower, he's going to be sixty-five this year, think of that, but for you it'll be like falling off a log, not even that, not even as much effort as it takes to fall off a log, I swear, the kid will meet you at nine, go through everything, you'll be out of there by ten..."

"By ten? I only get an hour to learn what you guys have been running for however long?"

"The kid's got to get out of there in an hour because he's got to get his ass over to the rehearsal, they're fixing something, which means they'll be a new orchestration tonight once they set the arrangement, but that's no panic, you'll all be in the same boat, and it's a rewrite of an existing number, so if you learn the one you'll be fine with the other, everybody will be fine. You know what these last minute things are like."

"Well, it's been a while."

"Jess, you're not going to flake on me, are you?"

"Flake?"

"Flake out. You said you'd do this, you said you're cool, so are you cool, I mean are we good to go here?"

"Yes, Richard, yes, I am, I am cool, but you have to understand I haven't heard from any of you in like fifteen years, more, and here you are on the other end of the phone giving me this gig, this major gig that starts like five minutes ago, I mean I can do it, I'll have to, I'm just a little out of practice..."

"What do you mean by that?"

"Nothing. I didn't mean out of practice. I mean it's just not what I'm used to anymore."

"You haven't been playing shows? Done any musical direction?"

"I haven't been in a pit orchestra in six years, and that was some light opera thing, two weekends. And as for musical direction, well, I don't know if it's because my name's not out there that much anymore or what, but I don't get asked to do it that much, most of the Equity stuff goes to Karen Dormer, she's half my age or a quarter of my age and everybody just loves her, so the rest of the stuff, the non-Equity stuff just doesn't pay that much, if anything, and it all goes to the college kids or the kids just out of college. What I'm saying is, I don't know what you imagine I've been doing since I left New York, but I'm sure if I told you you and Kay would have a good laugh or think twice about this offer which is maybe what you're doing now anyway now that I've told you I'm out of practice or just not in the daily habit of it or not out of practice but just without frequent opportunity, you know what I'm saying? I'm still adjusting to hearing the sound of your voice, Richard, if you want to know the truth, and adjusting to the fact that you had to dig my number out of the membership directory. I'm not saying there's any reason you should have me on speed dial or even in an address book if anybody besides me still has an actual, physical address book to write things in, and I'm not saying I'm not grateful, this is terrific, you're very kind, but you haven't once asked me how I am or what I've been doing with myself, or what I've been doing, although if you did ask me now I'd know you don't really care, you'd just be asking because I pointed out you didn't, and there's no reason, really, if you stop to think about it, why you should ask or care because everything's going great for you, you're assistant conductor on a Broadway-bound show, you're married . . . shit, I forgot about Lina. I'm sorry."

"Look, Jess, if you can't do this or aren't up for this, tell me, tell me now, because time's a-wasting and if you can't commit for whatever reason I need to start making some phone calls like thirty minutes ago."

"Who else are you going to call? I'll bet I was the last on your list."

"Now that's really rude, really uncalled for. In fact, you were the first person I called."

"Come on."

"God's honest truth. Now what's the deal here? Yes or no? I'm totally aware we've not been in touch, but you've got to understand life goes on, other lives go on, mine, Lina's, Kay's, everybody's, and nobody told you to leave New York, you just did, you just up and left, I don't know why, although I've a sneaking suspicion you thought things weren't going fast enough for you, you weren't getting enough opportunities. That may not be the case, but I know that's why Karl left, and Nelson after him to Los Angeles and then to Sacramento and now he's somewhere in North Dakota or South Dakota, one of the Dakotas, doing dinner theater. And Miranda, too, she stuck it out only so long and then said so long. I get it, it's tough, and yes, it's true, I have no idea what you've been doing with yourself, and it doesn't matter, I'm asking you for a solid here, I put out my neck for you based on everything from before, based on what I know of you or knew of you and your abilities way back when which, if you really think about it, isn't so long ago, fifteen, sixteen years."

"All I remember is the phone calls I'd get when I moved, the calls from you and Peter and Claire and all those other big shots, all those calls telling me I'd get a call if anything came up, how I couldn't waste myself out here, how I'd have to come back sooner or later, maybe to help out with Bill's classes or all those workshops or the readings and maybe even Lincoln Center, they always need somebody, you said, and then nothing."

"It's been tough for everyone. It still is."

"Yes, yes, I know, I'm not saying it hasn't been tough, and I'm not saying I'm special or privileged or anything like that, but I knew you people, we were tight, as the saying goes, we were living this all the time, and then to get nothing, not even a Christmas card or a wedding announcement or a referral down the line, maybe a call once a year on my birthday to see how it's going or what I'm working on..."

"Jess. Please. Stop. I'm sorry, I'm very sorry. I didn't mean to upset you. Look, we'll just forget I called, okay?"

"No, I'll do it. I'm in. Seriously."

"Are you sure? Because after all that…"

"Richard, trust me. I'm totally down with this, I can do it, I've just gone into panic mode what with the timeline you've outlined, but it's okay, I'm a professional, it's a Larriman score, what could be so difficult, right? And we all know how well I work under pressure."

"You're a rock."

"So tell me where I have to be and everything else."

"I'll call the kid now, give him your number, he'll call you and get tomorrow all set up."

"What's his name?"

"Jeremy something, starts with R. Come to think of it, he'll probably arrange to meet you at wherever they're rehearsing tomorrow morning, they can't get in the theater until the afternoon, but he'll tell you. As soon as I call him, which will be as soon as I end this call, he'll call you and you won't have to worry about a thing."

"Basic black?"

"What is?"

"To wear."

"Yeah, yeah, the usual drag."

"I'm sorry I got a little fussy there."

"No problem, I'm on edge, too."

"That's right, my God, poor Lina, oh, if anybody's got a reason to act crazy right now, it's you. I hope she's all right."

"I don't know what to expect, I'm going to get there, go right over to the hospital."

"Where's she at?"

"Sinai, of all places."

"Well, I'm praying for her, if that doesn't sound too weird, tell her I said hello and to heal or mend or whatever, even though she hates me."

"Lina doesn't hate you. Why would you say a thing like that?"

"I just assumed, because of you and me . . ."

"For the love of God, Jess, that's all ancient history, and she knows it, it doesn't even register with her, your name never comes up. Now look, I've got to go, I've got to call the kid, got to call Kay, Skip, my folks . . ."

"Yes, yes, go. I am mortified I've been taking up so much of your time."

"So, we're good?"

"Absolutely. And thank you. Thank you, thank you, thank you. Especially for saying I was your first call."

"I said it because it's the truth."

"One more question? Please?"

"Sure."

"Why was I your first call?"

"You want the truth?"

"Of course."

"Because I knew you'd be available."

"Ah."

"Jess?"

"Yeah."

"We're good to go?"

"We're good to go."

"You're fabulous. I'll keep in touch, let you know what the scoop is, and how soon I'm coming back. Oh, and break a leg. Or break a finger, as you used to say."

She hangs up, rubs her ear. She turns on the lights as the afternoon is darker than it should be thanks to the threat of snow. She cleans the living room, the kitchen, her bedroom, her bathroom, her music room. She finally gets a call from Jeremy something. She can barely understand him, he talks so fast. He gives her the address of the rehearsal hall, hangs up without saying thank you. She goes to her piano, a Kimball spinet several months past its yearly tuning, opens the piano bench and takes out Czerny's exercises. She makes a call to her manager at the car dealership and tells him she has to leave town for a few days due to a family emergency, her mother, hopes she hasn't used her mother as an excuse before, but she recalls she's never made an excuse before, and her manager is very concerned and kind and tells her to take all the time she needs. She thanks him a hundred times, hangs up, faces her piano and *The Art of Finger Dexterity*. She sits, opens to the first exercise.

She plays.

The Newly Discovered Unequivocal Origin of Baseball

Scurritt definitely was the first with the ball. It was something he fashioned without knowing. He looked down into his lap one summer evening and discovered he had unconsciously generated a thing, a round, hard thing, an apple-sized something or other over a series of warm and idle and tense evenings while sitting on his front porch with his wife. His wife, Molly, wanted to fashion a preservative cover for the object, as she is clever and sensitive with needle and thread. Scurritt lent her the marvelous sphere for this purpose, and she withdrew to bleach a swath of leather. One of us later remarked that the surprise wonder had been tainted once Molly was allowed to get her household hands on it. Compromised, someone else said. We could not fault Molly's handiwork, however, but that was not the point. It was then that Flaar took the ball from Scurritt and stripped it of Molly's covering. Flaar told us he would show us a sample of his own handiwork, and we did not see him again for well over a fortnight.

We have a certain amount of responsibility to ourselves and to each other and to our Mollies and to our families and to our communities and to our state and to our country. Buckstein is always bringing this up, this notion of responsibility. We discuss responsibility at his goading. He is a skilled orator once the whiskey has been passed around thrice. We recall how Scurritt's ball had moved him, and what he had said.

"This has nothing to do with God or Nature. This has everything to do with the two mighty legs upon which we ambulate and the two mighty arms with which we strike or embrace our young. We are gentlemen, gentlemen. We are gentlemen because not only do we endorse and encourage fairness we are also able to fairly judge fairness and recognize when we see it and apply it when it is warranted. Gentlemen, we are. We can. We do. We have the ability to use our eyes and ears and authority to exhort fairness. Fair play. Fair weather. Fairweather friends. That is not to say that we are friends. We are not friends, fair weather or foul. We are gentlemen. We are gentlemen who have responsibility. Who have ability. Who have power. We are a tried and true subsystem of universal system. But among each other? What have we? Responsibility. The wherewithal to demonstrate our gifts of fairness to our fellow gentlemen. We have that obligation. I say it is high time we took steps to show everyone what we know about ourselves and what we can do with that knowledge. We need something that shows this. Not a ritual but a sport. Not a ceremony but a game. Something we can play that says, See how fair we are. How organized we are. How us we are. See?"

Flaar returned and showed us Scurritt's recovered sphere. Crude stitches replaced Molly's dainty artistry. His skill lacked subtlety but we did not mind. Flaar's work made us aware of the seams, but we took pride in being able to recognize what Flaar had done and how he had done it. We were proud of its openness, its roughness, its honesty. It was a ball at its most basic, its baseness emphasized by its resemblance to a skull over which the white dead skin had been stretched. It was ours.

I tossed it to Burkstein. Burkstein tossed it to Galder. Galder tossed it to Walladanter. More gentlemen joined us, ten in total. They admired the ball. Culk cradled it. He said, This is the world. Porfett took it and said, This is our world. We nodded in agreement. Porfett tossed it to Niplinghaus. Niplinghaus did not catch it and it went through the parlor window. There was no embarrassment, no chastisement. A window can be replaced. We cannot. We needed to spread out. We needed a field.

While Galder cleared a portion of his field to be used for our tossing, Trunder appeared with the club. This club had the refinement the ball did not. The club was lean and smooth and finely wrought. We asked where Trunder had been all our lives. Trunder in his modesty said nothing. Culk took the club and said, This is us. Porfett took it and said, This is how we must be.

We had club and sphere. We moved from the parlors to Galder's field. We admired his skill at sacrificing a portion of his fine and fertile land for our displays of fairness and gentlemanliness. We gave no outward thanks nor paid no vocal compliments. We were who we are to each other. We did not remove our hats.

We gained another modicum of control over our lives. Not enough but nearly enough. We had the sun and the air and the soil and our ball and our finely refined club. We spoke and sang and joked and discussed and many times said nothing as we exercised ourselves with our newfound symbols.

We tired.

"Others need to know us," said Porfett.

"As viewers or participants?" asked Trunder.

"Yes," said Culk.

"They must begin as viewers," said Burkstein, "and progress to participants."

"Not participants," said Porfett. "Combatants."

"Not combatants," said Walladanter. "Competitors."

We went about our non-field moments pondering the question of competitors. Competitors, to us, meant Other Gentlemen. We had to acknowledge other gentlemen existed, and in order to find them we had to venture out into other communities, neighboring fields and parlors. We were wise and clever individuals, wiser and cleverer as ten on a field. We reasoned gentlemen everywhere had to be as we. It stood to reason. Word got out.

Other gentlemen appeared at Galder's field. They watched us as we tossed the ball and now and then used the club to make the ball irretrievable. The ball was always retrievable, but we tried to make it not. Burkstein held forth on this for all and sundry.

"To make it irretrievable is the key. We are wise and clever and know, naturally, that it can never be irretrievable, unless it was somehow sent into the middle of a pond, and even then, with some effort and ingenuity, it would be retrievable. No, as long as the Earth pulls objects back to its bosom by the divine method of Gravity the ball will always come back to us. But, as I said, this is not the key. The key is to make the attempt. The key is to face it as it bears down on you and make every effort to send it away from you. The further the better. Others will try to catch it. They might do this. They often will. But the key is to make the attempt to keep it away from others. This is the key. You must bat it away as you would a noisome fly. With power. And fairness, let us not forget fairness."

The other gentlemen, after a period of viewing us, asked to join our circle of ten gentlemen. We discussed fairness and responsibility and decided to accept them as competitors without telling them we saw them as competitors. This withholding of information could be interpreted as an example of unfairness, but it is not. We said *Let them think what they will think. If they are gentlemen, they will eventually arrive at the same conclusions as we.*

We invited ten.

On the eve of the first meeting, however, Burkstein, who had spoken to us so eloquently on every topic imaginable, died. He was found in his field by his wife, Molly. We mourned the loss of Burkstein, but not for too long. We had a meeting ahead of us.

We went to Galder's field and found the ten other gentlemen waiting for us.

"With Burkstein dead it will be ten against nine," said Flaar.

"That would not be fair," said Niplinghaus.

We told one of the other gentlemen to leave. One of the other gentlemen asked why we could not ask another gentleman to join our side. We told him it would be unfair to Burkstein, to the memory of Burkstein. It was he who first understood us and explained us to us.

"It must always be nine," said Flaar. One of the other gentlemen went away.

Eighteen, nine of us and nine of them, stood looking at each other, stumped at how to proceed. Galder, still grimy from maintaining his field's smooth playability, explained to the others that we used the game to reflect on our control of our worlds. One of the other gentlemen scoffed at this.

"This is not your world," he said. "This is our world."

"We can discuss that," said Galder.

"Discussion does nothing but waste time," the other gentleman said. Could he indeed be a true gentleman and make such utterances? Walladanter, who towered over everyone, stood midway between them and us. He was cradling the ball. The other gentleman was holding the ball batter, as he had been the first to admire Trunder's craftsmanship. Walladanter spoke to him.

"This is indeed our world," he said. "You are merely our guests."

We could no longer see our similarities. The other gentleman grasped the ball batter.

"This may be your home," he said, "but it is not your world exclusively."

"Say that again."

"It is not your world exclusively."

It was then that Walladanter threw our ball at him.

And the game began.

Essential Knowledge

The horrific drowning happens first and doesn't matter, as they continue to go, weekend after weekend thereafter.

The boys have basic names: David, Gregory, Michael, Henry, James, Stephen. The girls have old-fashioned names: Dorothy, Geraldine, Marilyn, Helen, Judith, Sylvia. It's thought their parents put little to no thought in naming them at birth. This thought is fact. They have the names of their great-grandparents, people nobody remembers well, if at all.

We encircle Henry with lighter fluid every time he falls asleep on the beach with a beer in his hand but the circle never lights.

There are the girls who wear bikinis, the girls who wear bikinis with t-shirts over them, and the girls who wear bikinis under their shorts and shirts. The boys leap around in their brown, red, blood orange, mustard yellow, and green swim shorts, except Gregory, who is on the fat side and never takes off his shirt. The girls and boys redden rather than tan.

No one asks Judith if she can swim.

As a child, she had been thrown into the deep end of her bachelor uncle's in-ground pool. She had paddled away from the shock, a fish in water.

James remembers.

Yeah, that was the summer I met that girl at Michael's house. Not Michael's house; no, we had gone from his house to somebody else's house—this girl's house, this girl whose name I can't remember. Not really a party, there were four of us: me, Michael, this girl, and some other girl. The girl I'm remembering was Spanish. Hispanic. Her skin was darker than mine. Not darker. More brown. Not like a tan. She was into cars. She had a vintage MG. I think that's what it was called. An old movie car. I think she said she had fixed it up herself. She was like nineteen, maybe twenty. She took me for a drive. Middle of the night, through the forest preserve, although that can't be right, you can't drive through a forest preserve. Well, there were a lot of trees and leaves, leaves on the ground, I mean. Leaves on the ground? Then it can't have been summer. Anyway, I wish I'd done something about her, wish I knew her name now. She was not one of the girls we usually saw, not one of the beach crowd. I wish she had been. The name Lucinda comes to me now, but I know that's not right.

They bring hot dogs and burgers, liters of pop, American cheese in individually wrapped slices, pickles, ketchup, mustard, bags of chips, buns, paper plates. David sneaks in beer. He can do this because he comports himself as older than the others. He isn't, but he knows how to present himself as older to the people from whom he wants to gain something. The girls take the beer, sip at it. Marilyn shivers. She is always cold.

Everybody hears Stephen's neck snap.

Stephen goes up the smaller dune for the fourth time, everybody laughing now. He strikes a gangly pose, sets off running. He comes to the edge, jumps, flails his arms and legs comically, a silent comedian desperate for an energetic laugh, falls short of the water, on his chin, dead halt, the rest of his tall, thin body continuing its journey, up and over his stationary head, nobody laughing now. Stephen remains in one bed or another for the rest of his life, useless from the chin down. The girls and boys visit, often at first, not so often eventually, hardly at all later. They always hear the snap, see the body do what a body wasn't designed to do.

The dark comes, or rather the deep blue evening. There is a fire, which took forever to light. Gregory is stingy with the Ronsonol; we're saving it for when Henry passes out.

Dorothy, always in leopard print, says to James "No, it'll hurt," and he says "Who told you that?" and she says "I'm sure it will," and he says "I was in the same health class as you; at no time did anybody say anything about it hurting," and she says "Can't we just sit here, nicely, and you can keep me warm, just hold me, maybe kiss me a couple times?" and he says "Said nobody, ever," and she says "I thought you were different," and he says "I'm not," because that's what he heard his father say a few times to his mother and one other lady.

Naturally, there is sadness about Judith. None of them had fished her out, and why would they? They hadn't been thinking about her or wondering where she had disappeared to. It was somebody else, a much older man, dripping and bow-legged, steely chest hair matted from the water, who brought her out and over to them. All of this happened after the food part of the day.

Geraldine remembers.

I did a lot of reading that summer although I can't for the life of me remember what all I read. Paperbacks, mostly. Stuff my mother had around the house, sex novels. Not really sex novels, but these stories about women feeling love and lust and contradiction and whatnot while the solid, gorgeous men they wanted behaved caddishly. Somebody's body would be caressed, you'd turn the page and it was inferred sex had happened. Oh, and I remember a line from one of the books, I don't know why I remember it: "He put his arms around her and felt, with pleasure, that her breasts were full and heavy." I guess I was disturbed by that. And mildly aroused, who knows why.

Helen stands at the water's edge, the shouts from the volleyball game behind her. She sees a light blue sky, a light blue lake, each light blue its own version of light blue: calm above, movement below. She looks at the horizon, searches for it. It's right there. But it isn't. She thinks the lake is a mirror of the sky, but a mirror that shows the true nature of what it reflects, and if that is so then which of the two halves is the true reflection? The sky or the lake? This is the only time in her life when she will stand apart from the others, distracted, looking out, thinking, calm and disturbed.

Oh, how we soak the sand around Henry's unconscious figure.

Judith and Sylvia watch David scamper. Judith says "He has no ass," and Sylvia says "None of them do," and Judith says "Gregory does," and Sylvia says "Like a dump truck," and Judith says "But David," and Sylvia says "They're all so skinny, always pulling up their pants," and Judith says "No hips," and Sylvia says "I hate them," and Judith says "Me, too," and Sylvia says "What I mean is *envy*," and Judith says "Yeah," and Sylvia says "Marilyn looks so stupid."

Stephen remembers.

It was all about movement; mine, in particular. We exploded that summer. We'd park the cars and just orgasm all over the beach, climbing up, rolling down. Tossing things around. Tag, something we hadn't done since we were kids. When we were younger kids, I mean. Simple stuff. Running ahead, right into the water, stopping short, risking a soaking. Getting soaked. Damn cold water. When we looked at each other, we saw breasts, navels, nipples, abs. God, how I wanted what's-her-name. I don't think the burgers were cooked long enough. Didn't matter. We worked everything off, didn't we? The fat? I was over-aware of my feet, my elbows. I mean the bones therein. Barefoot and shirtless all day. Michael had square toenails. I think it was Helen who first noticed, when we were all sitting around. The toenails on his big toes were square, and when we saw this, when our attention was drawn to this, we were fascinated.

Michael says "That's just the way they are," and Gregory says "Then you're a special case," and Michael says "Maybe I am," and Stephen says "Oh, you're a special case alright, a mental case," and wings the football at his head.

Michael remembers.

Yeah, that was the year I had to have surgery because I had ingrown toenails and it got pretty bad. The surgery was okay because I couldn't see what they were doing and they gave me a Walkman to listen to. Yeah.

The girls are stretched out, sunglasses on, coated in suntan oil. The boombox is pulsing something they all know extraordinarily well. The boys are figuring out the cooking.

Somebody tells them drowning doesn't always look like drowning. This scares the hell out of James, because he's just started lifeguarding off Lake Shore Drive, and while he sees (as he puts it) "a lot of fine-looking tail" while on duty, he quits. If drowning doesn't always look like drowning, what good is he? He starts at Foot Locker the week after Judith is buried.

Gregory remembers.

It was me who figured it out because one night I wasn't as drunk as I wanted to be. It was the sand, you see. Of course it wasn't going to light. I think, originally, we just wanted to make a ring of fire around him, like a big, fiery crime scene outline. That would've been a riot. And he'd wake up surrounded by these flames, you know? And we would laugh our asses off. But, you know, sand? Basic science, but there we were, wasting the lighter fluid and the stuff we brought for the grill. You kind of forget the essential knowledge when you've been drinking. Well, not just when you've been drinking, but when you've been running around in the sun all day, just doing goofy shit, eating everything in sight, lusting after whomever, leaving trails of shiny, slick hormones all over the place. All the common sense sort of dribbles out of your ears, you know? Well, it was me had the bright idea, once sober, that if we wanted to light him up, we should actually pour the stuff on him, not around him. And it was like a half-dozen light bulbs went off over a half-dozen heads.

The girls always sleep as they ride home, except one, who watches everything they pass, the contrast between dark places and light places, the people she won't ever know, walking, biking, running, ordering burgers and slurping through straws, shouting, fighting, laughing. The noise of the light and the quiet of the dark.

Stephen thinks *My head's come off.*

Dorothy says "Oh, and it hurt, it hurt like an emmer-effer, just like I knew it would. Oh well."

Henry wakes, smells something delicious, realizes it's him, leaps up, flaps like a shocked phoenix, runs for the water, dives in, everybody laughing.

Judith swims, floats, listens to the peace. She finds she is sleepy. She falls asleep. That is all.

Husband Technique

Stremple is here because it's 10/10/71, which means yesterday was my twenty-ninth birthday (sympathy cards are still being accepted) and I'm a single woman (see prior note about sympathy cards) with my own apartment who's listed in the phonebook and can't get a good night's sleep. Stremple has his own life (I like that about him) and I wanted to cook for a friend and women don't cook for other women, at least none of the women I know, so he's over tonight, for a variety of reasons. The phone rings and I tell Stremple to be prepared, but it's only my mother with Happy Birthday, a day late and a dollar short, so I roll my eyes and tell her I'm cooking and I'll call her back later, and when I hang up Stremple is looking at me sideways from the breadstick he's crunching, his eyebrows up to his hairline. He's never met my mother but he's heard plenty about her and he knows when not to say anything and I tell him to stop standing so much, sit down, sit down.

The next time the phone rings it's Heavy Breathing, and I can't really use the Husband Technique on Heavy Breathing. I hang up. Stremple asks if I mind if he dips a heel of bread into the sauce and I say sure it's what I do anyway when nobody's looking, which is all the time. He says it smells delicious, but I can't be sure he smells the right food.

I live two floors above the pizza joint on Ridge, a couple of blocks away from where Hollywood makes its startling jog to the right to pursue a lazy Northwest route through the city and into Evanston. The shiny-skinned, golden Mexican boys who work in the pizza joint always have a greeting for me when I come home, like someone's rolled out the free cerveza, their floury fists in the air as the dough hovers over their paper hats. I've never tried the pizza or walked in— the joint is small and the tile yellowed with unwashings, but the warm, aromatic fog that saturates my old building always keeps me hungry. Stremple has remarked that he, too, is always starving the few times I've had him over, how he's thirsty, too, and at the moment he's doing a great job of lightening my gallon jug of Gallo (he's awfully cute; I just wish he'd either shave regularly or grow the damn beard already). He sits on my kickstep stool and watches me, his eyelids fluttering with each long inhalation of wine. The phone rings.

"Hey, Leigh, how's about a little you and me tonight?" the caller asks. My ears go hot and I snap my fingers at Stremple to get his attention. "Let me have you talk to my husband," I say, "maybe I can sneak away if he says it's okay." I pass the phone to Stremple, but I've heard the click before he can say hello.

"You could just hang up," he tells me.

"Hanging up never discourages them," I say. "Husbands, however, do."

"All these cranks want is attention. Don't give it to them."

The thing is, I always know when it's a crank, because cranks call me Lay when my name is pronounced Lee. Friends know me as Lee. Anybody doing business with me knows me as Lee. Some whacko trolling for names in the phonebook sees Leigh and thinks Lay, and I get the calls sodden with lust.

Stremple shovels his way through the spaghetti and meatballs and I follow suit and afterward we wonder what the hell to do with ourselves. It's one of those damp early October nights where the streets are glistening even though it hasn't rained, and neither of us are interested in any of the movies that are showing. He asks if I've got any games and I say Scrabble and Parcheesi, but I'm not sure I have all the tiles for the former and never really learned how to play the latter (it's something my sister left behind). We put on some records and sit in my box of a living room, killing the wine. The phone doesn't ring.

"I wonder if I should practice my husband voice," he says. He thinks he ought to sound august, rumbling; the tones of a three-piece sober suit and a leather briefcase. He practices. "This is the husband," he intones like a radio announcer, and I'm laughing. The record changes, we wait; the needle digs the grooves and the music is perhaps a little too relaxed because Stremple asks if I want a back rub.

I'm immediately aware of my boobs because my top is tight, not because I wear tight tops but because I've packed on a few pounds since moving up here, maybe because I've been breathing in the pizza joint and have loaded up on the calories through osmosis, but I can't go into the bedroom to change into something looser like my pajama top because that would send an even more invitational message and I deflect him by saying I'm too tense for a massage, I'd break his fingers off. He doesn't press the offer, taking me at my word.

The phone rings, and a new voice says, "Did I wake you?" I snap my fingers at Stremple; he shimmies over. "No," I say, "but you've interrupted some world-class sex between my husband and me. Here, he'll confirm that." But before I can pass the phone to Stremple, the voice says, "My husband and *me*," and hangs up.

"It doesn't help to engage them," Stremple says. "Be dull. It's your best defense." He's always got advice for everything (I like that about him), but he doesn't come off as a know-it-all (Ibid.), like my brother. I drink the last of the wine. We stare at the shameful emptiness of the green glass jug. "I should fill that up with pennies," I say, "like my grandfather used to do." Stremple is distracted by the smeared view from my windows and I can't imagine what's so interesting out there. "I think he wrenched out his back trying to lug his bottled pennies to the bank once," I continue. The phone rings. "Let me answer it," Stremple says. I let him. He barks a sharp hello and then passes the phone to me. "Your mother," he says.

What follows is a long explanation of not so much what a man is doing in my apartment but who the man is and how long I've known him and what does he do for a living and was something romantic being interrupted. I suffer through the call, as Stremple had the good sense to remove himself to the kitchen to attend to the cleansing of the dishes that would have otherwise gone uncleansed by me until at least the weekend.

It's late and quiet and we could, if we so desired, turn over the stack of records and listen to the B sides for another couple of hours, but once he's stacked my dishes in the cabinet above the sink and upended the wine glasses on the so-called drying towel, he's shrugging into his jacket and saying he's got to get up early. He's lingering at the door and my arms go all pimply with a sudden chill. I know it's late, but it could be later, and, soon enough, it will be, and that's when the fun really begins. The most disturbing calls come during the swampiest hours of the night, always when I've slid into a dream I won't remember. If I don't answer, the phone rings and rings, and once I'm up, I'm up, and that's when I need Stremple. He's placid and lovely with a brittle ruggedness and I don't know what I'm saying. My bed, topped as it is with every conceivable blanket and pillow and wedged into a comforting corner could easily accommodate two, if the two are locked in a protective lateral hug and don't move around too much.

But his hands are hidden in the pockets of his jeans, and I'm opening the door to let in a damp wave of oregano and pepperoni. He gallops down the steps, thumping past the door of the fat old lady below me. I bolt my door twice, firstly the original vintage contrivance that came with the apartment, secondly the shiny, new, blocky, battle-ready bolt Stremple had installed before our quiet dinner.

An hour before dawn, the phone rings. A voice says, "Listen, Leigh, either you do everything we say or we're coming over there to rape the shit out of you." I want to say, "If you're coming over, pick up a pizza downstairs on your way up, no anchovies." I want to say, "Well, raping the shit out of me might solve this constipation." I want to say, "Define everything." I want to say, "My husband will be happy to let you in," but I don't have anyone to whom I can pass the phone. Be dull, I think. I say nothing. I can hear myself breathing. Because the caller called me Lee, not Lay.

Pamachapuka

The Stelladders have a nice living room and dining room facing the street. On the second floor, there is a master bedroom and a small study that can be a guest room if there is a guest, but they do not sit in any of their rooms looking out the windows at the boulder or at anything at all because to them the outside is a nice background and nothing else. This is how it is for them. The boulder weighs 570 tons and never bothered anybody until it moved.

The Lenape Indians who used to live in the region had a name for the boulder: Pamachapuka, stone from the sky. This was the only way they could explain its presence.

The Stelladders were grateful for it because it served as a good landmark for people trying to find the house. Just opposite the Pamachapuka. Then they had to explain, and it made them feel very local. It is a good thing for the children to play upon if they are careful but their children are growing up and do not bother with it anymore. It is also a good backdrop for family photographs and there are plenty of now in the photo albums. It is huge and amazing and haughty, and it moved.

The Lenape Indians who used to live here had no idea no concept of glaciers and how they once travelled all over the globe. That is why the Pamachapuka is here. It rolled over a glacier a long, long, long time ago.

I am certain it moved, the wife said.

Impossible, the husband said.

Look at it when you leave for the office.

I'll look but I'm telling you it didn't move, nor did anybody move it, nor could they.

I'm telling you it moved.

Then the husband pulled the car out of the garage and backed down the driveway and swung into the street. He looked at the gigantic boulder for quite some time because Mr. Vatocik drove up behind him in his pickup and waited for a little before he honked his horn. The husband returned to his driveway and Mr. Vatocik sped away.

It moved, the husband said when he went inside.

Told you, the wife said.

This upset them. They sat in their living room and thought about how to explain their discovery for a long great while.

How does something get to be where it is? Sometimes you will encounter something so alone in its otherness that you can only assign mystery to it. No matter where you are in time. These very big natural things you encounter are beyond human strength even though we can pretty much do whatever we want in this era of oomph and conceit.

What I'm striving to say is: T.L. and I have been married for nearly five years next week and I'm fairly certain she's made a discovery but is keeping it from me or keeping it to herself which is the same thing but not entirely. The question is why she would do something like that? I'll return to this.

The Stelladders thought long and hard into the afternoon. The wife became concerned that the husband hadn't gone to the office or called in and they hadn't been answering the telephone.

If the Pamachapuka didn't move that means we did, the wife said.

Impossible, the husband said. Stop calling it that.

What should I call it?

What it is—a big heavy rock.

Fine.

When something that size moves there's usually a sound or it leaves a trail around its base, like the earth being shuffled. There's no trail and we heard nothing.

I suppose the same goes for our house.

Exactly.

So there's no evidence of us moving and no evidence of the boulder moving.

Correct.

But it moved.

I know.

You should call the office.

The Stelladders were unhappy because they did not have any answers. Their children came home from school.

Who moved the rock? they asked. The wife readied dinner.

The Lenape Indians consider a Pamachapuka a gift from above. It is a big rock where there are no other rocks and so it is very special and anything that special must have a meaning and purpose. Early settlers in the region used the Pamachapuka as a mile marker and a signpost. Natives and intruders judged their existence in relationship to the Pamachapuka. A more modern scientific term for Pamachapuka is erratic. Erratics can be found everywhere.

T.L. and I perhaps need to spend some time apart. We work together and sometimes it is a wonderful and convenient thing to have married a fellow scientist and that way there is always something to talk about at dinner. We do things the old-fashioned way and in that way we are now considered somewhat retro by colleagues, but we are careful and the only way to be careful is to do things the old-fashioned way and then put everything into a computer.

T.L. and I work with the sun.

We have an observatory at the top of the house and in the morning we fix the telescope and open the end not pointing to the heavens and we get our pencils and pens and start drawing the images of the sun on large paper. We are Carringtons in this respect and I don't want to get too technical but in essence we are on the lookout for another solar superstorm like the one Richard Carrington tracked in 1859. This has little to do with the deep down of T.L. and I at this point.

Drawings are clearer than photographs and always have been. People pay us for all of this. T.L. defers to me on shading and I defer to her on diametrics. We are complementary is what I'm striving to illustrate and work together independently at the same time and because of this it is impossible for her to make a discovery without me making the discovery as well.

But she has.

The Stelladders' eating is at first secondary to their contemplation of either the Pamachapuka or themselves in motion without leaving a trail. It is a fact that the quietly inexplicable can put one off one's food although the children suffered no ill effects and, in fact, asked for seconds, which they received, and then thirds. The Stelladders think it would have been preferable if the wife had only imagined it. The husband wishes his wife would not have drawn his attention to the phenomenon.

Let's not say anything about this to anyone, the husband said.

If we noticed it and the children noticed it then other people will notice it, the wife said.

So what if they do? It's not our fault.

Maybe that's what it is, a hidden fault somewhere rolled it a little or us a little.

So now you're a scientist.

Don't snap at me.

Well then let the whole world notice it, noticing things doesn't explain them.

Maybe we should call off the bridge party tomorrow night.

T.L. and I listen to our favorite classics while we work and she's partial to amateur composers like Borodin who was a chemist and Carpenter who was a businessman while I am partial to the composers who couldn't do anything except compose like Bach and Beethoven and Mozart and a whole bunch of other big names. I mention this because T.L. is now taking a shine to my music as this morning she asked for a partita and I obliged. She has discovered something I haven't and she is not telling me. I construct a list of reasons why T.L. would do this:

T.L. does not want to become famous all by herself because she loves me.

T.L. could tell everyone that we both discovered what she discovered because she loves me.

T.L. is waiting to see if I will discover what she has discovered because she loves me.

T.L. has made a major minor discovery or a minor major discovery, which means that either way no one's life is threatened by or dependent on it and so she can afford to keep it to herself until bringing it to my attention. This has nothing to do with her loving me.

It has everything to do with patience.

It has everything to do with having one up on me so that if at some future point I behave in a way that she does not like she can remind me of my imperfection as a human being and a scientist by revealing her discovery.

This doesn't sit well with me.

If I made a discovery that T.L. didn't make I would tell her immediately because I love her.

Or do I?

Why do I tell her anything?

When the Lenape Indians put their hands on the Pamachapuka, they felt a heavy vibration coming up from the Earth and into the stone and that is why they left it alone.

The Stelladders did not cancel the bridge party and the Alts enjoyed the cocktails and the cheese and pimento loaf shaped like a four of spades and the bowl of little snacky things. The Alts did not notice that the Pamachapuka had moved or that the Stelladders had moved. The husbands in fact got a little high on the martinis and one wife had to drive her husband home and the other had to shoulder hers up to bed.

They spoke over breakfast.

I'm still trying to figure out how you knew it had moved, the husband said.

Something felt off, the wife said.

With the rock.

With everything.

And that made you look outside.

I just happened to glance over when I brought in the milk and the paper.

I'm still trying to figure out how the kids knew it had moved.

If you're trying to say it's only my imagination and the only reason you see it as well is because my power of suggestion is strong…

Not so loud, I've got a hangover.

The Alts didn't notice it.

Thank God for that.

So the noticing is limited to us, to our family, the four of us.

Or so it seems thus far.

What does that say about us?

I don't know what you're implying, now let's forget it and how's about some more coffee.

T.L. doesn't need to encourage me to talk about anything that is on my mind because that is something that goes unspoken. I could come right out and ask her, but I know how the conversation would go.

Have you discovered something without telling me?

No.

Or:

Have you discovered something without telling me?

Yes.

T.L. is very matter-of-factual in that if a question asked requires a simple affirmative or negative she will supply the simple answer and go no further. Her comeback is always: *You asked me a yes or no question and I provided the appropriate answer.* This is what gets me. How am I to know that she did indeed provide the appropriate answer? T.L. is very good at debating the meaning of appropriate and by very good I mean she doesn't tire as quickly as me. I won't ask her right out because she will think I've become suspicious and we need to work together beautifully as we always have the many years married and not that we have loved each other.

When the Lenape Indians figured out that they weren't wanted in the region anymore they departed. To take the Pamachapuka with them would have been impossible. Their horses were strong but all of them together could not have moved the erratic stone, which had fallen from the sky for a reason and its reason was not to be altered by anyone.

College kids did it, the wife said.

There's not a college around here for miles, the husband said.

This is not my fault.

Well don't make it mine.

T.L. is humming along with the Bach now and she is very happy.

Each day you will look at things differently than you did the day before and not because you planned to look at them differently. I am referring to the erratic outside our house. I am looking at it and thinking why in this era of strength and certainty has nobody moved it to take advantage of the land. Perhaps it is the cost of moving such a monolith even though I have no idea what the cost of such a prospect would be. I don't want to move it. It lends a certain timelessness to the neighborhood even though the neighborhood is just our house and the street and the forest preserve behind the erratic. It reminds me that it was here millions of years before T.L. and I and will likely be here millions of years after T.L. and I are gone, although even that is not so certain in this era of convenience and ability.

You've been staring at that rock all morning, T.L. says.

I wonder who discovered it, I say.

Impossible to know.

Because it's so old.

Because it has nothing to do with us.

So you're saying things like that are never discovered they just always are.

It moved once a long, long, long time ago and it won't likely ever move again.

A glacier moved it.

Well then a glacier will move it again someday—now are you going to do any work this morning or is it all up to me?

The Stelladders are last seen in front of their house. The husband pounds a wooden FOR SALE sign into the lawn and the wife pulls up her grandmother's rosebushes and the children are off playing somewhere.

T.L. is very good at what she does and no matter what she does I can't explain here I can't explain why I'm still here doing the same things alongside her and converting her to my composers and I will likely never figure out what she is keeping from me, if she is indeed keeping anything from me.

The glacier melts. The boulder rests. Some winged creature too new to be named sees the boulder and it alights on it and while this massive rock will not make an excellent home it does make a nice place to rest for now.

The Disappointers

He watches the movers lug the headboard up the stairs. He says, "Take it easy," but they don't hear him or pretend to not hear him. He's going to have to paint over the marks they just made on the wall. Suzy comes in. She holds a big box. He says, "That bed's too big for that room," and she says, "Is there a problem?" and he says, "I don't know where you got that bed, but I'm telling you, it's not going to fit in that room," and she says, "I measured everything before. Excuse me." She goes up the stairs. The movers start to come down. They notice she can't see over the big box she's hefting so they back up to let her up. She turns down the hall, they watch her ass. They smile, come downstairs, go out the door.

"Another disaster," he says to his wife in the kitchen. She says, "What is?" and he says, "Knocking into everything," and she says, "Who is?" and he says, "Those thugs she's got for movers," and she says, "They break something?" and he says, "Not yet. What are you doing?" and she says, "What's it look like I'm doing?" and he says, "Fixing a sock," and she says, "Then that's what I'm doing, only it's called darning, not fixing, not that you would know, you can't do anything for yourself," and he says, "That's uncalled for," and she says, "Why don't you busy yourself somewhere else? Go down the block for a beer," and he says, "Somebody's got to hang around, see what else she drags into this house." The front door bangs. He says, "Jesus! I want to leap out of my skin every time they bang that door," and she says, "Well, if you'd've fixed the thing when I told you, the thing that you can adjust to hold the door open, you wouldn't be leaping out of your skin," and he mutters something she can't hear and doesn't look up when he goes back to the front hall.

He catches Suzy coming down. He says, "I thought you said you only had a few things," and she says, "What's the problem?" and he says, "Every time I turn around they're dragging something else in here," and she says, "Then don't turn around so much," and he says, "Very funny, but you kept telling me you only had a few things," and she says, "I do," and he says, "A few is two or three things, four at the most. Already I've seen a bed the size of an Oldsmobile that's not going to fit in that room," and she says, "It fits," and he says, "Then the room is going to be all bed, I don't see how you're going to fit anything else in there," and she says, "Do you have enough beer for these guys?" and he says, "Beer? What are you talking about?" and she says, "Karen and everybody else told me it's a good idea to not only tip the movers but to give them beer, too," and he says, "That's horseshit," and she says, "And I didn't pick up any beer," and he says, "Well, they're not getting any of mine," and she says, "Can you run out quick and get me some, maybe a 24-pack?" and he says, "You've moved around plenty of times the past couple of years, how is it you forgot to pick up beer for the movers this time around?" and she says, "I've had a lot on my mind," and he says, "I'm not running out for anything. They want beer, I'll send them down the block to Kedger's or over to the CVS. It's ridiculous, giving them a tip and giving them beer on top of that," and she says, "I forget the last time you moved was in 1967 when things were done differently, but today isn't 1967 so maybe get with the program a little." She goes out the door. He goes down the block to Kedger's.

It's Kedger's oldest son tending bar that afternoon, the son with the one milky eye over which he wears an eyepatch. Gordon. He says, "She the one who's the big doctor?" and Frank says, "She studied to be. Didn't finish," and Gordon says, "I thought she was a big doctor now. You want a shot with that?" and Frank says, "What time is?" and Gordon says, "I think it's two or a little after, or a little before. Definitely in the neighborhood of two," and Frank says, "Yeah, give me a shot of rye," and Gordon pours him a shot and says, "Well, tell her Gordy says hello, if she remembers me," and Frank says, "She couldn't remember to go to all those classes years ago, how's she going to remember you?" and Gordon says, "It's the other one who'd remember me, your older girl, Kathy," and Frank says, "Karen," and Gordon says, "Because I was just a year behind her. She's a big lawyer now, last I heard," and Frank says, "Not anymore. Turn on the ball game, would you?"

The movers finish the beer. They say thanks and leave. She says to her mother, "You think he'll notice?" and her mother says, "How many'd they have?" and she says, "A couple," and her mother says, "How many are left downstairs?" and she says, "Maybe a half dozen," and her mother says, "He only goes near that stash at Thanksgiving or Christmas or when your brother visits, so I wouldn't worry, but pick up some as soon as you can just in case," and she says, "That's expensive stuff," and her mother says, "That's not my problem, it wasn't me gave them the beer."

"She wasn't so bad," the bigger of the two movers says to the other. The other says, "You got a thing for older women," and he says, "She wasn't so old," and the other says, "So ask her out," and he says, "Should we go back?" and the other says, "To do what?" and he says, "So I can give her my number or something," and the other says, "Forget it," and he says, "I think she was checking me out," and the other says, "She was checking both of us out. That type always does. And what would you stand to gain by asking her out? Middle-aged woman living with her parents? You'd be footing the bill for everything, and she'd always end up at your place for the night and not cook you breakfast because she's the type that can't cook to save her life, and then she'd hustle you into giving her a ring, and once that's out of the way she'd tell you about some kid she's got stashed away somewhere. Of course she was checking you out. You were wearing pants," and he says, "Did you see the size of that bed?" and the other says, "Wishful thinking on her part, that's what I say, and it looked antique, if the both of you got on it you'd bust it for sure," and he says, "I guess you're right," and the other says "Take it easy on the speed here, it's a school zone."

She's on the phone with her sister. She says, "He threw a fit because I had the movers take the bed that was already in there out to the porch along with the long bureau that was Aunt Julie's or Aunt Nancy's, I forget which," and Karen says, "He doesn't like change," and she says, "No, he likes change when he's the one changing things," and Karen says, "That's right," and she says, "I sold off what I could, but I couldn't rid of the bed, not that I wanted to get rid of it, it cost me plenty and it's great," and Karen says, "The mattress?" and she says, "Yeah, the mattress, but the frame part, too, it's all the same thing when I say 'bed,'" and Karen says, "Well, you survived three weeks already. If that's all he's had to moan about, everything else is velvet, right?" and she says, "Oh, he moans about everything. Last night it was because I was in their room watching television," and Karen says, "On that dinky set they've had since we were in high school?" and she says, "The very same," and Karen says, "What was wrong with the one downstairs?" and she says, "They're always in front of it. And we don't watch the same programs. Oh, and they've only got the basic cable. I might as well be living on the moon," and Karen says, "Hey, at least you don't have to worry about the rent," and she says, "Yeah yeah yeah. Only I don't remember them being so critical about everything. Mom got on my case because she said I was washing the clothes all wrong, and I told her I'd been washing my own clothes at one laundromat or another for the last twenty-five years, and she said her machines were different, and I asked her how different, and she said she'd just do all the laundry herself," and Karen says, "At least you offered," and she says, "Yeah, although I'm telling you that dryer's on its last legs. It rocks like you wouldn't believe. You start up a load, come back an hour later and it's halfway across the laundry room," and Karen says, "Does she shove it back all by herself?" and she says, "She must," and Karen says, "Of course, she wouldn't ask him to do it," and she says, "God forbid," and Karen says, "Well, hang in there," and she says, "You too," and Karen says, "I'm trying," and she says, "What's wrong?" and Karen says, "I'll tell you later, I got another appointment tomorrow. These doctor bills are what's going to kill me, not the colitis."

It's Kedger's middle son tending bar that night, the scrawny one with the red hair now going silver on the sides. Nicky. He says, "No, there's nothing wrong with that, we still do it at my house. It's a dying thing, maybe, but we still do it at my house," and Franks says,

"And yet I tell her we're not running a restaurant and she gets all bent out of joint," and Nicky says, "I don't know what to tell you. I was raised same as she and that's what I teach my kids," and Frank says, "How many you got now?" and Ricky says, "Just the two," and Frank says, "Why'd I think you had more?" and Ricky says, "That's my brother Wyatt. He's got like four or five," and Frank says, "And I thought three was a handful," and Nicky says, "Say, how is Adele?" and Frank says, "Who knows," and Ricky says, "She don't come around much?" and Frank says, "Doesn't know what a phone is, either," and Ricky says, "She's a big actress now, right?" and Frank says, "Who knows," and Ricky says, "I look for her on television, I never see her in anything, except that one shoe commercial, but that was a while ago," and Frank says, "Yeah," and Ricky says, "You hear from her, tell her Ricky says hello," and Frank says, "And speaking of saying hello, how's your old man doing?" and Ricky says, "He don't know anybody anymore."

They're in bed and she says, "We can make the adjustment," and he says, "Who's going to do all that work?" and she says, "When the movers come we'll have them move everything that's in the den into the big bedroom," and he says, "That's my office," and she says, "You never use it as an office," and he says, "There's the desk in there, and that nice rolling chair I picked up at that sale, and all my papers," and she says, "You have to go through those papers," and he says, "I'm in the process," and she says, "You've said that ever since you retired but you never look at any of that crap," and he says, "Let's get back to this Karen thing instead of right away being so critical of me," and she says, "Nobody's being critical of you," and he says, "I just want to know where she expects us to put all that stuff. We've got the sofa and those two end tables, the three lamps, that foot-stool, my recliner, that antique table next to the recliner where my magazines and the clicker are, plus the entertainment center and the television. How's that going to fit upstairs in my office with the desk in there and the two bookcases and that futon Kenny had in college plus our old kitchen table I also use as a desk?" and she says, "We'll just have to move things around," and he says, "There's still that bed on the porch and my uncle's old bureau," and she says, "Well, that's one thing taken care of, or two things, actually, because Karen told me she's bringing nothing. We can set up the bed and the bureau for her in the den," and he says, "Is she going to be comfortable in the den?" and she says, "I wish you'd have a little sympathy for her and her condition instead of moaning about where all this stuff is going to go. The den's the best situation. She can't do stairs, so your office is out, even though it used to be her and Suzy's room, and so is the basement for the same reason. With the den converted to a small bedroom, she's right around the corner from the powder room and the kitchen, and she'd have some privacy because of those partition doors that haven't been closed in who knows when because they didn't need to be closed," and he says, "What's she going to do for a bath?" and she says, "Bathe, of course," and he says, "All the powder room's got is a sink and a toilet," and she says, "I forgot about that."

"You like bowling?" Jim says. Suzy says, "I haven't been bowling in a thousand years," and he says, "Neither have I, but I thought it'd be something to do," and she says, "Anything to get out of that house," and he says, "We don't have to bowl all night. They've got a lounge," and she says, "Oh, I know. Are you good to bowl?" and he says, "Why not?" and she says, "I just assume your back's got to be always hurting because of all the lifting and carrying you do," and he says, "No, I'm in shape, I try to stay in shape, and also that's why I wear that belt," and she says, "Still, it's got to be tiring work," and he says, "They stick me with the short jobs, the easy stuff, the two-guy jobs. And if there's a bigger load there's usually three or four guys total, and then I let the younger guys haul the big stuff while I get the boxes and smaller stuff, although sometimes that can be tough because people don't know how to pack books," and she says, "Well, that's one thing I didn't have, all those books," and he says, "Where do you work?" and she says, "I'm still looking."

She's on the phone to the nurse practitioner. She says, "It's probably because we still haven't figured out the bath thing yet," and the nurse says, "Well, what have you been doing?" and she says, "Well, every morning my mother brings me this old washtub from downstairs and I have to make do with that. Like a sponge bath thing. And once a week, usually Saturday night, my sister helps me upstairs and they put a shower chair in the shower and I'm able to clean myself pretty good, only I'm so tired after I have to stay upstairs until the next day, and the futon up there is too low for me and my sister's bed is too high so I sleep as best I can on this rolling chair, but it's not very restful," and the nurse says, "Maybe we should get a home health nurse out there," and she says, "I can't afford that," and the nurse says, "I'm sure your insurance would cover it," and she says, "I doubt it," and the nurse says, "Don't you have disability?" and she says, "It's coming, I'm told," and the nurse says, "Can't your family reconfigure the downstairs bathroom? Expand it to include a shower?" and she says, "We've had that discussion, and there's nowhere for it to expand to. They'd have to expand it into the kitchen and then there'd be no place to sit in the kitchen. Even so, the whole setup of the bathroom would have to be switched around because of where the toilet and the sink currently are. And my father nearly went through the roof when we talked about it," and the nurse says, "There's got to be a better situation," and she says, "This is it."

Mrs. Glenhurst says, "Well, it sounds like you have your hands full," and she says, "And Frank is the worst. Always fuming about something," and Mrs. Glenhurst says, "I've never known him to fume," and she says, "He fumes all the time now, is always uptight. Spends a lot of time at Kedger's," and Mrs. Glenhurst says, "Speaking of, I hear Bill Kedger's doing real bad," and she says, "Frank didn't tell me," and Mrs. Glenhurst says, "Well, men don't talk about those things. Well, would you look at that?" and she says, "What?" and Mrs. Glenhurst says, "The way she drove off, didn't take her cart back. And that thing's going to roll into somebody else's car," and she says, "Where's the cart lady?" and Mrs. Glenhurst says, "Patsy," and she says, "Yeah, that's her name. Come to think of it, I haven't seen her the last couple of times I was here," and Mrs. Glenhurst says, "I think she died or else was doing really bad and had to be put in a home," and she says, "Poor sweet girl," and Mrs. Glenhurst says, "The stock boys're supposed to come out now and round up the carts, but they don't, not often enough," and she says, "Well, you take care," and Mrs. Glenhurst says, "You too, and tell everybody I said hello. At least it's a help to you with Suzy around, I mean a help to Karen," and she says, "Oh, Suzy never finished her internship or whatever it's called," and Mrs. Glenhurst says, "But she must have some medical knowledge," and she says, "She never brings it up. You know, it's awful hard being a doctor. All that work before you become a whatever-they-call-it, where you can start your own practice. She explained it all to me once, I got exhausted just listening," and Mrs. Glenhurst says, "Well, good luck with Karen," and she says, "We need it. I'll let you go; I've got ice cream here that's probably all melted by now."

They leave the bowling alley lounge and he starts to take her home but she asks if she can stay over at his place.

There's somebody new tending bar he doesn't recognize; maybe it's a grandson or nephew.

She loses her balance in the shower and sits down too heavily and the chair cracks and she goes over backwards and dislocates her left hip.

The dryer rocks itself so far from the wall it unplugs itself, ruins the outlet. Sparks from the outlet land on the old rag being used to stop the gap between the water pipe and the wall, a small fire breaks out and goes out in the space of two minutes. The washing machine short circuits, blows a fuse, sends half the house into darkness. He has to call somebody in.

Kenny sends new pictures of the grandkids.

The phone rings.

She calls upstairs to him but gets no answer. She goes upstairs. He's asleep in front of the television. There's so much furniture in the room she can't figure out a way to reach him, and the television's on so loud. She gets his attention on the fourth yell. She says, "It's Adele on the phone, she wants to talk to you," and he says, "Why can't she talk to you?" and she says, "She's in trouble," and he says, "Money?" and she says, "I think it's maybe worse than that," and he says, "Have her talk to Karen," and she says, "Karen wasn't a criminal lawyer," and he says, "She knows enough law to help her out," and she says, "Karen won't get out of the hospital until next Tuesday," and he says, "So give her the number at the hospital," and she says, "I haven't got it," and he says, "Have Suzy deal with her," and she says, "She's out. And she borrowed the car," and he says nothing because he knows but does not want to say aloud that he will have to do something, again, something to straighten things out, something something something always something, and he is tired of doing something and besides in order to leave where he's at he will have to dig himself out of the mess surrounding him and he doesn't know where he's going to find the strength or the space to shift everything around, but she's not leaving the doorway and he's already missed a couple of crucial minutes of his program thanks to his nap and now this intrusion, and he thinks that's how it is and this is how it's going to be only it will get worse, and he doesn't necessarily feel old as much as he feels emptied.

He says, "Okay. Give me a minute."

The [Some Girls] Assignment

Some girls might think we are heroes because a bunch of people we never met are going to be killed today.

As always happens before any of our mandatory and questionable sprees someone is going to cock around in an attempt to make us laugh and we will laugh not just the first time but the second time even a third time but after that you're pushing it. Cresp is the clown of our band and he's pushing it now. There is only so much funny that is funny and we all try to be funny because let's face it we are in sore need of funny because not much is funny but as everyone throws down with funny there is a certain democracy to it but Cresp on the other hand just wants attention. We give it to him. We take it away when he pushes it. He gets the message then but only for a couple of hours and then he's off again with the funny. The thing is when you are like that you get to have a reputation.

I've been told to write one thousand words about this but I don't think that's going to happen. I think I might write more than one thousand words anyway. It is impossible to write and count words at the same time or maybe it is not impossible but it's damn difficult. That last sentence is twenty-two words and this is ten if you don't count the hyphen, nine if you do, and look now it's twenty-five. If I can manage to keep my sentences down to ten words and write one hundred of them this will all be over.

Some girls have deep thick voices and they are typically tall and keep their hair long and are either totally into fucking or don't want anything to do with it.

We all agree that after Cresp makes a fourth funny he has pushed it and Solt shuts him up good. Solt is not the biggest of us but he is big enough and he is not the meanest of us but he can make a point with a good shove.

None of us slouch. We have been badgered into superior posture by our superiors who have also helped us through rigorous exertion to build mighty fine bodies that women drool over when we are allowed to see women which is not ever but they'd drool if they saw us. Fivarito takes pride in sharing with us a letter he received from his wife in response to one he sent to her with an enclosed photo of himself in his new outstanding physicality and his wife wrote *When you get back I'm going to wear you out or die trying.* Fivarito always says to that *Now there's a reason to come back alive* and he says it over and over and over and over. We don't like it when he says that because we don't like the words he chooses which is to say we don't like those particular words strung together but we don't say anything to him about it. Anyway we all think Fivarito's wife is a bit of a whore even though we have never met her or seen her we just know.

I have to write this out with my hand and my handwriting is tiny and packed and I could care less if they will be able to read it, they will have to bend forward to see it and possibly squint and really look really really look and that's a good image to have in my brain, them having to really really put forth some effort to read this thing.

Birnes has yet to grow into his face. Birnes is the youngest of us and it is still possible to imagine him crooking a slim arm across a Mead notebook as his neck reddens as he talks to the tall girl he is studying with. His teeth are too big for his mouth and he licks them and I think he still thinks he is wearing braces. I'll bet they were newly off when he signed up and shipped out. Birnes is an obvious virgin and I think his virginity bothers many of us but for once it is a botheration we do not discuss. Birnes sleeps an untroubled sleep which surprises and angers all of us because we expected him of all people to be an antenna for nightmares. Cresp says this untroubled slumbering is a sure sign of virginity and Solt says it is a sure sign of a history of playing video games for hours and hours and hours and Fivarito says that makes him feel safer and we leave Birnes alone when he sleeps. Somebody among us should sleep like a baby.

Some girls are short and squat and develop early and wear tight striped tops and when they drive a car they prop their unoccupied leg up against the door and at the movies they put your arm around them if you haven't already done so.

We are very aware of the clock and the door. The clock is big and its size is a comfort. The clock is one of those clocks you might see in a factory or in one of those control rooms where everything depends on everyone seeing the same clock and it makes a humming sound and none of us look directly at it we glance at it in secret. We will sit and talk. Our muscles are shelves and our guts are rocks. We will edge forward a little while talking and sitting and make it look like we are about to stand but we don't we look up at the clock. The door is a door and is always shut except when it opens and when it opens it means something and that is all that can be said about the door.

Many of us miss sweet coffee.

There are several hundred words now if not one thousand and maybe I can be done with this even though I have not written about what I have been told to write one thousand words about. I smell a skunk which is impossible there are no skunks here so the question now is what smells like a skunk but is not a skunk. Cresp is being funny about it first time second time third time boy is he pushing it.

Some girls are very young who are very young not because they are very young but because their bodies are turning not very young and they know it but don't know what to do about it what to do with it yet and you would like to show them.

We are very hungry today but do not eat much.

I have asked them why they want me to write one thousand words about what will happen and I was told it is an order and I accept that. I think however I think many things and maybe what is wanted is a prediction about the immediate future but all future is immediate so that is a stupid thing to say. A prediction about what will happen based on what did happen what happened many times before oh yes many many times before. If that is the reason then one thousand words is way too much. Thirteen words would cover it nicely. Thirteen words. Less with editing. Too late now.

There are things we do not discuss three come to mind and these very few three things go untouched by Cresp although he can find the funny in anything and everything. But we do not let him because we do not let ourselves. We talk about girls and back home.

Back home to all of us is small and big. Back home our towns and back home our country. When we say back home we mean all of it, small and big and our towns and our country. Very few of us are from cities. Breek is from a city. Breek is no different from us and I'm not implying that he is trying to fit in but his stories about girls are without passion and seem kinkier. We do not question his stories. We listen to all stories many of them the same stories over and over and over and over and we listen without complaint and none of us care if they are the truth or fantasy and even if they are fantasy that's okay that's understandable. We cannot prove fantasy. How can we check the facts of fantasy and how can we know if someone is lying and it doesn't matter it is the story it is the stories that are there and they are welcome. Except Birnes who tells no stories because he has not lived any stories because he is waiting to have some to have just one.

There is a hush now because none of us are saying anything.

Some girls have a tattoo on their foot and these girls often take birth control pills. Breek tells us this. Everyone nods and everyone understands. Birnes is napping. We want to wake him up but Birnes should sleep because we think he should do the sleeping for us and the dreaming too.

Solt makes as if to stand up but he does not he glances at the clock. Behind the door are all sorts of sounds and smells and some of them we recognize and some of them we do not, which makes it very hot where we are inside, waiting to go outside.

Fivarito is telling me that when he closes his eyes he can still see shapes and this is possible for someone who has thin eyelids. I am telling him I have never heard of such a thing and it is the truth I have never heard of such a thing. Fivarito is closing his eyes and is saying Try me. I hold up three fingers in front of him and he is saying Three. It is unsettling.

We are hearing a collection of footsteps outside and someone is asking Cresp to say something funny and Cresp does not for once. Fivarito opens his eyes. Birnes is awake and his neck and cheeks are red.

We are dressed for it we are armed for it we are trained for it we are prepared for it we are nonetheless wishing it was not about to happen. Something will happen. To us. To them. We hope more of it will happen to them than it will to us. We hope.

I would like to tell you what all of us are thinking, but it would be the same thing over and over and over and over. I will try. We are thinking make it through make it through make it through make it through make it through. We are thinking now now now now now.

I would like to tell you how comfortable we are and how uncomfortable we are in our clothing; it is all the same clothing, we are all the same.

I would like to tell you how heavy we feel.

I would like to tell you how it feels to be very aware of your own neck your own nape your own back of your head.

I would like to tell you how each time before has been and then maybe you will see the unnecessity of what I am writing now, of what I have been asked to write one thousand words about, but I can't.

Some girls make you perspire when you hold their hands. These are the girls you love.

I have lost track of my one thousand words and anyway it is time. I will choose the thirteen essential words those thirteen words that are all I need to write oh yeah I will choose them later when I get back and we'll see if I can get away with that. We'll see.

They'll owe it to me.

Empathetics

Some people can live their entire lives without imagination and we know some of these people. Some people can live their entire lives submerged in their imagination and we know some of these people. Some people can live their entire lives on a limited imagination and we know some of these people. Some people can live their entire lives as products of the imagination and we do not know any of these people.

GSS and I venture out in our own personal blackouts after one day because with the bandages around our eyes it is difficult to be sure of anything let alone the time of day. I say bandages because what we wear are more than blindfolds. A blindfold in GSS's opinion is not a very good word. She admits to the folded portion of the word but not the blind. She can see she said yesterday when we began and I said I can see too and that was it as far as tradition was concerned. We had called up Trenker and explained our difficulty and our plan and our desires and Trenker had obliged us by appearing with ocular padding and gauze and bandages and tape and Trenker is always so helpful and so thorough and so uncurious.

GSS falls down the stairs even though I told her to wait for me to go down first in case she should fall and then I could break her fall and when I tell her this she tells me she thought I had indeed gone down first and I ask her if anything is broken and she says no but she can only speak for herself. I am slow I am moving in swim-like fashion I am all outstretched hands in front of me. I am so very very very aware of every part of my body every inch every joint everything I have I am thinking and naming everything as it moves—heel of hand palm fingers on wall knee first then heel of foot, then soles then toes, everything has a name.

Some people can live their entire lives pretending. Some people can live their entire lives pretending sometimes. Some people can live their entire lives pretending certain things but not certain other things. Some people can live their entire lives not pretending anything.

The ocular padding nestles in the caves of our eyes without pressing upon our eyes. The gauze is a trifle itchy and buffers the ocular padding from the bandage. The tape is of the surgical variety and it anchors the gauze and the ocular padding and tugs at the crow's feet at the tired corners of our eyes. The bandages python around our heads thrice and are clipped into place. We are satisfied. We cannot see a blessed thing.

I case the stairs inch by inch. I sense a great uncertainty in front of me. I know that if I take a spill down the stairs as GSS has that I will probably not meet my death but even that is uncertain as some people can fall down a flight of stairs and survive and some people can fall down a flight of stairs and perish. I call to GSS and tell her not to move and she tells me No problem. I paddle the air. I search for that first step down. I find it and it is toe then toes then sole then heel then ankle and the rest of me moves forward part by part and I do not let go of the wall the dear sweet stable wall and here is the right banister the left should be to my left but it is not.

GSS explained to me We have to make this believable. GSS asked if I knew any blind people. I had said no. I said I had seen *The Miracle Worker* on cable when I was a teenager and I'm sure a couple of other movies had blind people in them since then but I couldn't think of the names. GSS told me she could walk around with her eyes closed but she would cheat. GSS does not believe in cheating. I recommended the blindfolds. The blindfolds let in light somewhat and we could cheat by looking down for a sliver of sight of motion. GSS told me there are some people who do anything for their craft. I told her I considered us among those people. GSS told me there are some people who always know and knew they were that sort of people. I told her That's us.

I have an idea and I tell it idea to GSS. I tell her it will take me forever to centimeter down the stairs and it will be faster if I grab the left banister and slide down to wherever she is. GSS tells me to try it. Without losing touch with the friendly wall I bend my knees and lower my ass to the landing. I slide over to where I hope the left banister is by always reaching always swatting at the air until I find it. I hoist myself up onto the banister and suddenly become sick.

Some people can live together and never see each other by choice. Some people can live together and never see each other by circumstance. Some people can live together and never be able to live untogether. Some people can live together.

GSS and I before venturing out spent a formless, eternal, experimental day in darkness. Not just darkness but blackness. Not just blackness but bottomless void. It was not an absence of light although it was and it felt like an absence of placement an absence of grounding a complete negation of relationship. Within minutes it became clear to us that everything in the apartment was now our enemy. Our bodies became more intimate with furniture. GSS asked me why we have all this stuff. I said to her Imagine if. GSS said Yes imagine if. I said to her It would all be arranged differently. GSS said Definitely and less of it.

I call to GSS and tell her I am very sick and she does not answer. I tell GSS that I'll be right there but am frozen to the spot. I cannot relax my grip to let me slide down the banister. The polished century-old wood is my ice flow, my buoy, my raft, my rock, I cannot cannot cannot bear to part with it. I call to GSS that I'll be right there and she is still not answering. I sense a chasm to my right. I feel that if I move so much as one atom I will go toppling into nothing. I call to GSS that I'll be right there and I know she won't answer.

We had decided not to move around so much and confined ourselves to the floor of what we assumed was the living room. We passed the time by searching each other and that was fun for a moment and then it was exciting and then it was arousing and then it was inventive and then it was serious and then we faded to black just like in the movies when two people have gone from fun to excited to aroused to inventive to serious to sex.

Some people can live their entire lives alone and we know some people like that. Some people can live their entire lives alone most of the time and we know some people like that. Some people can live their entire lives having conversations that go something like this.

I wonder what time it is.

I can't even guess.

How do people who are like this all the time know what time it is and do they even know what Time is?

I don't know.

It must be late.

It can't be that late.

I wonder if you can feel Time.

I suppose you have to listen.

Listen to Time; is that what you're saying?

Listen for Time.

Listen to what.

Outside. Street traffic.

So you are saying street traffic can help you feel time if you can't see time.

I suppose I am saying something like that.

I think I understand. Street traffic is heavier at certain times of the day.

And night.

Rush hour.

There are two rush hours.

What if you live on a main artery where the traffic is always heavy?

Like we do.

Exactly.

Well maybe you have to feel for sunlight and by that I mean if you can feel light on the floor or heat from the light on the floor then you know it's day and when you don't you know it's night.

What do you do on a cloudy day?

Where are you?

I'm right next to you.

How close?

Feel.

Further away than I thought.

That's spooky.

I don't feel any light.

I perspire and the perspiration is cold. I am certain that if I try to let myself slide down the banister I will fall something will happen

I will fall to my death I will plunge into the greater darkness only I know it is not an empty endless darkness there is something down there more stairs and that will be it for me.

GSS calls Where are you? I tell her I'm right here. GSS says Further away than I thought. I ask her Did you pass out? GSS says Possibly. There is nothing between us for a long time and GSS says Why aren't you here already?

It had taken us forever to get dressed after our seriousness as we had not taken care to remember where our clothing had gone. We patted the floor. We tried on things that weren't our own. I ripped something. GSS struggled on the floor like an electrified fish with what I assumed was her pants. We had exhausted ourselves. We were hungry. We had lost track of the kitchen. We crawled on our elbows. We slithered across the floor. We met walls. We met tables. We broke a lamp. We elbowed into the pieces of broken lamp. We cried in pain. We did not give up. We salamandered over every mile of the apartment. GSS said How dirty this floor feels. The floors were cool and gritty and I could somehow taste them in my mouth. We found the refrigerator. We were too tired to open it and begin foraging.

Some people live their entire lives without saying it was worth it. Some people live their entire lives saying it was worth it. Some people live their entire lives not even thinking about worth.

I want nothing but sleep. I want to put my hot cheek on the cool banister. I want to fall.

We were left to ourselves and our bodies and wondered if we had been foolish to wonder how it would be. GSS said We can't conclude anything yet until we are out in the real world. I said Just say world because real is implied and in here is not the unreal world you know. GSS said We are learning so much. I said It is not happy learning.

GSS snaked away. I called to her, Where are you going. GSS said To find the toilet and drink. I said Make sure you flush first. A long time later I heard a flush.

GSS tells me You have to come down I can't seem to get myself up. I breathe new hope. I tell her If you are hurt after all and need help I won't be of any use because I can't function and maybe I should we should start yelling for help. GSS says We have to do this for ourselves we have to we need to be self-sufficient. I tell her That's bullshit everyone needs help regardless of their circumstances. GSS tells me Don't you dare yell help. We are on our own here.

Some people can live their entire lives without anything happening to them and we know some of those people. Some people can live their entire lives without knowing their neighbors and we know some of those people.

Some people can live their entire lives without a scrap of light and we are now those people oh yes we are now those people by choice.

I let go.

Notices

Every last one of them on both sides of it felt somewhat betrayed by the whole thing at one time or another.

Most of them took their seats less than three minutes before curtain. All of them remained seated during intermission, none of them fraternizing. All of them cleared their throats during the second act, despite the theater's warmness. All but one of them left before the curtain call. The one that stayed only stayed for a few seconds into the applause, looking for a lost glove.

The producer's gofers brought the newspapers to the party several hours later, one by one, fresh from the street. Everyone at the party was smashed. They sobered up the second they heard the rustle of the notices.

Felder had chosen to spend the bulk of the words on the scenic design and its execution, particularly the innovative use of the turntables and what looked (to him) like cellophane.

Kurenblitt had come up with new mountains of praise for the leading lady, misquoting her best lines left and right.

Sherbst spent ninety percent of the allotted space dissecting and bemoaning the current state of the American theater scene before warning readers away from the production.

Huke waxed rhapsodic over everything and everyone involved in the purplest of prose known to modern criticism.

Gernitsch compared the piece to everything the playwright had written over the past fifteen years of her career and found it falling somewhere in the middle of her achievement.

Wemberley admitted to being neither enthused nor bored.

The party ended.

All of them returned to their apartments, homes, or hotel rooms. One said to another, "So?" The other said, "So what?"

"Which is it?"

"Which is what?"

"I mean is it good or bad?"

"I don't know. Depends on which hit home for you."

"Well, the good, naturally."

"But?"

"But…"

"But the bad things hit deeper."

"Of course they did."

The next day, the leading lady sent Kurenblitt a note of thanks. She scented the note with rosewater. The rosewater blurred the ink in one crucial passage, and Kurenblitt arrived at her hotel room the next afternoon, much to her horror. She pushed him off of her. He showed her the note. She corrected the line. He blushed brick red up to the roots of his remaining hairs. He left. She laughed, hands trembling.

The producer was one of the first people to hear of Sherbst's heart attack upon turning in her copy. He sent flowers to the hospital. The hospital phoned to say Sherbst's heart attack had been fatal. The producer muttered over the wasted expense of flowers and sent a gofer to retrieve them, if possible, to send to Sherbst's funeral, if any.

The supporting players played endless, listless hands of rummy between performances. They had nothing to say to each other because none of them had been mentioned in any of the newspapers. "It's a star show," one said. "It will run as long as she's willing to do it," said another. "She's not known for long runs," said another, "and nobody wants to see her understudy." "Who is her understudy?" asked another. "I am," said another. "Gin," said another, fanning out her cards.

Mrs. Albert Carr of West 65th Street asked four of her closest friends if they wanted to see it. Two were indifferent, one was enthusiastic, and one didn't care either way. "I heard it was good," one said. "I heard what's-her-face is great," another said. "I heard the scenery's nice," another said. "I heard it was lousy," another said. The five of them went to a matinee and were intrigued until a certain point and then their thoughts left the action on the stage and went somewhere else: the evening's roast, the weekend's bean supper, Nathaniel's bar mitzvah, that dress.

The playwright took a call from her agent who had taken a call from Hollywood. "Not that studio," she said. "They completely botched *The Humble Basin*." "I got news," the agent said, "that's the only studio that's called." "Wait another week," the playwright said. She rolled two sheets of paper sandwiching a carbon into her typewriter. She typed ACT ONE then LIGHTS UP and heard the impersonal clang of the machine echo throughout her apartment.

Miss Helen McMurlan of Omaha, vacationing with her aunt and uncle, saw the play and had her life changed forever. Her aunt would forever remember her niece's white-mittened hands clutching the playbill, cheeks rosy with discovery and November. "Oh, wasn't it the most wonderful thing ever?" asked Helen forty-three times on the way back to the hotel.

Felder hated musicals and sent a second-stringer to cover the musical comedy opening later in the week while he sneaked off to the movies. The producers of the musical comedy complained long and loud about this, but Felder lived it down. The musical comedy went on to enjoy a long and profitable run.

Wemberley was hired by a television network.

The leading lady's leading man never spoke to each other except when onstage together and speaking lines written by another that they had rehearsed. The leading man said to his wife, "Listen, don't get too comfortable here, this will run but it won't run forever, and then it's back to Beverly Hills." His wife said, "I don't see any reason why you need to go to all those understudy rehearsals; isn't that what the stage manager is for?" The leading man said, "What, and have me walk out there one night to act with a total stranger? You want me to ruin everything?"

The producer looked at the first week's receipts and said, "We can keep this going another two months, maybe three if we keep running the quotes about her and that other stuff about the play itself, but I don't know." He reached for the telephone, bit off the end of a cigar.

Many hurried under the theater marquee without looking up at the show's title or the leading lady's name. Snow and slush were getting into their boots and shoes, wind was howling down their necks.

Months later, the awards people had to refresh their memories. Oh, yes. It wasn't good or bad, it just…was. I liked it. It was okay. She was dynamite, but I saw it early on. There was that neat thing they did when the hotel became the church, on a turntable, yeah, but also the way they whooshed the thing up into the whatchamacallit. Oh, yeah. I loved it. I thought it was the worst piece of crap (pardon me, ladies) I'd ever seen, and if it hadn't been for that third martini I had at intermission, I would've left. Oh, I think people underestimated it. Oh, I think it was horribly overrated. Oh, I think it deserves something.

"The trouble with mixed reviews," one stagehand said to another, "is nobody who reads them knows how to act."

"Yeah," said the other, "I noticed that."

"A big fat hit is one thing; everybody goes around like it's the Armistice, and there's candy and flowers and telegrams and lots of fooling around in the dressing rooms."

"Yeah. I noticed that when I was pulling ropes for..."

"A real flop is another thing; everybody packs up and gets out as fast as they can without another word to anybody, like a Schnauzer trotting away from a freshly shat pile of shit."

"Yeah. I noticed that when I was hauling the flats for..."

"But look at these poor dopes. They don't know how to act. It's not a flop, it's not a hit, it's... it's whatever everybody wants to think it is."

"Yeah. I noticed that."

All of them put the show on their resumés and listed it in their future biographies.

Mr. Paul Frencza of Queens managed to snag a poster on its last performance and obtained the signatures of everyone in the cast except the actor who played the priest in the second act.

Gernitsch actually took the trouble to see it again and write another piece about it that nobody really read because the show was going to close anyway.

All of them felt differently about it as time went on and as they grew older and as their memories faded and nobody, not anyone anymore, was around to remember what it was really like, what its worth was or was not, what the truth of it all truly, truly was.

Division of New Hope

We are married for a goodly time and then we are not.

What is surprising is how young we are when it is all said and done or should I say when it is all yelled and done. We are finishing while our friends are beginning. We were bright new pennies minty and minted fresh when we had decided to attempt that which our timeworn friends are only now attempting. Marry young. It is still done or at least it was still being done when we did it. Youth is a welcome mat she tells me and she also tells me we never wiped our feet. I tell and have been telling others, these friends, that our young marriage came about because I wanted to prevent her from being eaten by alligators and there is much truth to this despite all the laughing. We originated as Southerners in all our white trashy glory and gradually migrated to Yankeedom and that is perhaps why we are still young after enduring so long together.

But this isn't about our era of non-eternity and starry-black-eyed-ness. This is about our work in the Division of New Hope.

We continue to see each other every day except Saturday and Sunday because our paychecks come from the Division of New Hope and our offices are at opposite ends of the grand, echoey, waxed and ringing Third Floor. Most often we are reminded of each other in passing. We nod as others nod or split a flat good morning. We sit at the same long, smooth table on the last Thursday of every month. I see reports that betray her authorship and she sees ones betraying mine. She is occasionally assigned to one of my teams or I to one of hers where neither of us are the leader. We are professionals which is to say that we are naturally how we are to each other and are not performing and there is no tension. Those who work with us have no idea we are no longer married because they did not know we were married. My name is very common and she took it and this name is so common that three others on our floor have it and so you see we weren't special after all just shareholders of a few letters of the alphabet. We could be siblings. We could be cousins. We could be anyone.

But this isn't about the adjustments we never needed to make. This is about our work in the Division of New Hope.

Recently on a field exercise she asked me if I had met anyone.

I meet people all the time.

You know what I mean.

I do and therefore my pretending I do not would seem to indicate that it is none of your business to begin with.

All right then do not answer my question.

The only reason you asked the question in the first place is because you yourself have "met someone" and you want me to know, therefore, by asking me you think I will ask you in return, which saves you from coming right out and saying it.

And by taking great delight in your windy deduction you answer my question after all because if you had "met someone" you would have answered yes to begin with.

Unless this game of verbal tag we are now playing is my way of saying this is hardly the sort of conversation one conducts in a professional setting.

I still conclude you have not "met someone."

I meet people all the time.

I must mention at this point that there is no reason why she and I should not and could not be meeting people in the way she means and she means romantically. I am forty and so is she or at least she will be three weeks from Tuesday and she is still quite lean and active and treads gently and I am of course heavier but it is solid heaviness and one side of my haircut is splashed with silver and I am told it is most distinctive and sexy.

But this is not about our retention of our youthful unchildrened bodies or our current market value. This is about our work in the Division of New Hope.

You are no doubt aware of the Division and its purpose so there is little I can add to that. Let me point out that in the work we do at the Division of New Hope she has and always has had a completely irritating way of collecting information while in the field. She cannot help but ingratiate herself with the families we meet. She behaves as if this ingratiating manner is inbred but it is not nor can it be to anyone in our line of work. Watch her sometime. It is a trick of the neck and tilt of the chin and children and adults are won over. I should say watch the people she interviews rather than watch her as it is always the case that you can learn more about a work of art by watching anyone react to that work of art than you can by looking at the work of art itself. In this way you will see that her effect, that is the effect she has on everyone except me who sees it for what it is. You can see that she causes the same sort of reaction children in Kenya display when watching Charlie Chaplin for the first time. The gleam from the exposed, happy teeth could blind you.

I cannot call her out on this because it is not overtly an overt thing and there is nothing in our code that says we cannot bewitch our research. My secretary once let it slip during a lunchtime lapse into candor that people are only intimidated by things they cannot do and people they cannot be. My secretary is a very wise lady almost fifteen years my senior and is most adept at the xerographic machine and even though she speaks well enough and wisely I believe she got it incompletely. I believe we are irritated by the appearance of comfort in others when there is none in ourselves. That is intimidation.

I am not saying that I am or ever was intimidated by she who used to share my bed and breakfast nook. I am making an observation of how she is able to achieve something that no one else can achieve and there ought to be a law against it.

Every now and then I am required to have a word or two with her after the morning prayer.

Good morning. I have received an invitation to so-and-such's wedding.

I have not.

I know.

Because they still think we are yoked.

It is not my fault if your friends cannot remember the slightest things.

Slight is right.

I will not rise to that.

Very well.

I merely mention this because I assume you will not wish to be seen with me.

You are mentioning this because you don't want me to come with you.

I did not for one moment think you would be seen with me.

I am seen with you now.

We are in a professional setting.

You can be such a child.

I may not go myself.

Then give me the invitation and I will bring a guest.

The invitation clearly invites us and does not invite one or the other with the enjoinder "and a guest."

Give me the invitation.

Here it is.

Thank you.

You have ripped it in two.

I'll take my half and you can take yours.

You are obviously the one who is behaving like a child.

I'll either see you there or I won't.

But this is not about our labored negotiations and reterritorializing. This is about our work in the Division of New Hope.

My secretary has taken to saying things like there are no shades, people either do something or they do not do something. She is almost completely correct. I believe people either choose to do something or they choose to not do something. I tell her one word I tell her Choice. Choice. Choice. It is all choice.

We see each other on Saturdays and Sundays now because business is being forced to boom and there are more of us and there is great urgency and we have been issued blazers the color of picnic sunshine. You cannot miss us.

She believes in our work and I believe in our work and we have been with the Division for a goodly time and we are for the most part looked upon as stalwarts and we can answer any questions you might have. She has taken to letting her hair grow long and chestnutty and I have been learning that I cannot have dinner with ladies fifteen years my junior. It is not the great canyon of years that is bothersome it is the small cracks in flexibility. I am expected to remember everything I say and wish and want and not only remember it all but to never swerve. I am constantly reminded that I am a contradiction and this did not seem to matter before. I am learning that I am still improvising and I do not understand why nobody values improvisation anymore. Perhaps nobody ever did and she and I were unique in that that was all we knew how to do. We knew how to not do things.

On the day I screw up the courage to ask I be relieved of fieldwork I find that she has already asked and been granted leave from fieldwork. I throw myself into fieldwork. I am earnest in my research and quick. I am a dynamo.

Q: Do you foresee a change?
A: Not really.
Q: Do you want a change?
A: Definitely.
Q: Can you imagine a change?
A: Sure.
Q: What are you willing to do for that change?

A: What are my options?

Q: Answer the question if you please. What are you willing to do for that change?

A: Whatever you say.

I am a fountain of work in my dazzling coat and my still young self. I devise new questionnaires and leave them breathless.

Q: Do you know the meaning of happiness?

A: Happiness is being happy.

Q: Since you do not know the meaning of happiness are you willing to be told the meaning of happiness?

A: Sure.

Q: And once you learn the meaning of happiness would you share it with others?

A: Of course. Except my cousin Jeff, he's pretty much a douche.

Q: What if I told you it is not happiness that we're after?

A: It's not?

Q: Answer the question.

A: I'd be confused.

Q: What if I told you it is new hope we are after?

A: I would wonder what the new hope is.

Q: Something better than the old hope. Something that improves upon the old hope. Something that makes the old hope look like despair.

A: Sign me up.

I see her skirting the glossy hallway as I approach. I see her without her blazer. I have no invitations in my pocket. I have no memoranda to pass along. We are weeks away from the next long table meeting. I have nothing.

I take to returning to where I live and sitting in the one comfortable chair by the window with a single lamp burning over my shoulder. Some nights I fail to remove my blazer. I am interested in the little slice of world I see from my window. I watch the plunging of the buildings into darkness, the springing of the interiors into light, the slivers and crescents and slices and cookies of the moon. I stop coming up with ways to improve the work we do at the Division of New Hope. My imagination has exhausted itself.

I see her sitting outside her own office and ask her if she is waiting to see herself.

Don't be an idiot.

I trust all is well.

You may trust.

If all is not well I hope you know I am all ears.

Oh, I'll bet you are.

I have not seen you in the field.

That's because I've not been in the field.

If you do not wish to talk to me then say so.

I don't want to talk to you.

My secretary waters my plants and says things like roots grow deep unless the plants are in pots. I do not correct her.

Q: Do you like this coat?

A: It's awful bright.

Q: Doesn't it cheer you up?

A: It's ugly and annoying.

Q: Really?

A: You look like a goddamn life raft.

Q: Perhaps I am.

A: Look, I'm busy.

Q: Wait, wait. Are you aware of the work we do?

A: Vaguely.

Q: And?

A: I think you're fools.

Q: We're trying to convince you.

A: Of what?

Q: Of whatever it is you need to be convinced.

A: I don't need to be convinced of anything.

Q: You can't just give up.

A: Too late.

Q: Too late? Then how do you survive?

A: What kind of questions are you asking?

Q: The wrong ones, it seems.

I see her next in my office.

Listen, I told this guy I met, this really nice guy, I told him I'd had an abortion.

But you've never had an abortion.

I know but that's what I told him.

I am still trying to figure out why you told a really nice guy you had an abortion.

I felt it was better than telling him I fell.

And now I am trying to figure out why you are telling me all this.

Because for the first time in my life I've figured out how to lie.

Oh.

I mean lie without provocation.

There must have been provocation.

No, I don't think so.

Then what do you think.

I think he was a really nice guy and I should get out of here.

As our numbers increase and our fieldwork expands there is resistance. This is a shock to all of us. We had been doing so well. My secretary is let go. I am forced to do everything myself. The xerographic machine does not like me. We are asked to return our coats. We wear our own clothes. We have meetings at the long table every other day. She is no longer there.

Q: Do you foresee a change?

A: Why not? Change is inevitable.

Q: Do you want a change?

A: We've already had a change, a big one.

Q: Can you imagine a change?

A: Once upon a time I didn't know what to imagine. I was of the mindset that everything was bright and new and perfect and whatever was going to happen to us would just happen and that would be exciting. It wasn't so much about things changing, it was about things flowing. I don't suppose you'd understand. Although you did, once.

Q: And what are you willing to do for that change?

A: I didn't answer your previous question.

Q: Then answer it.

A: I can't answer your questions because we're not really listening to the answers. We never did.

Q: What if I told you it is new hope we are after?

A: I'd wonder what the so-called "new hope" is.

Q: Something better than the old hope. Something that improves upon the old hope. Something that makes the old hope look like despair.

A: We didn't despair. And don't say we did. We just didn't know what we were doing. But at least we're young, we're youngish, the roots don't go that deep, do they, even after twenty years? Because we were young and are still young? Right?

Q: This is not about us. This is about the work we do in the Division of New Hope.

Which closed last Friday.

Tour of Nothing

LBH and I drive somewhere anywhere does it matter it doesn't matter not to us not really lately and we see a great expanse of nothing no different from the other great expanses of nothing we've been seeing ever since we left the city. What makes this particular great expanse of nothing so unlike the other great expanses of nothing is what looks like an ice fishing hut at its edge upon which hangs a large hand-painted sign that reads TOUR OF NOTHING—EVERY HOUR—$5—EST. 1964. I think What in the blue hell and LBH must be thinking What in the blue hell too as she tells me Pull over so I pull over.

Then I think Wait a minute this is how people get killed people get murdered like this just pulling over for no reason in the middle of nowhere there are killers just banking on the random puller-overers. So forceful is this thought that I say it out loud and LBH tells me Like we had planned anything better to do. LBH digs in her purse for something. Her camera. The car crunches over a gravel drive which umbilicals from the highway to the tour hut. Behind us on the highway trucks knife along at top speeds.

We approach the hut or booth or whatever it is. A rusted Ford pickup hides behind it. In front is a clean economy car of anonymous make anonymous to me because I know nothing about cars except how to drive them and occasionally lock my keys inside them which is why I carry two sets of keys although today I can't remember where I left the second set. A man and woman of uncertain ethnic origin lean against this nice economy mystery car and a little boy appears at least I think it is a little boy and I think the little boy belongs to the ethnically ambiguous couple. I ask LBH if this is really what she wants to be doing and she tells me, Anything to get me out of this car.

I park at a respectable distance from the family or trio of uncertain people for no other reason than this is how I operate I mean this is how I park and observe the rules of strangers I park decently enough away from others so as not to risk scratching of paint or denting of bumpers or entrapment or a whole list of car-related woes and hassles. I say to LBH, Who in their right mind wants to take a tour of nothing and she says, These people obviously. I check the time and say Assuming "TOUR EVERY HOUR" means every hour on the hour we've got another twenty-three minutes to kill. LBH says, Whatever.

It wouldn't be fair of me to mention now but I will anyway I will mention that LBH and I are currently at a loss as to what to do with each other. When the weather is nice there is only so much sidewalk eating you can do and when the weather is not nice there is only so much television observation you can do. LBH is not from here which is to say I am a native and she isn't so she can't fool me with surprises like innocently planned trips. Last summer she told me to take a Friday off work and pack a suitcase for the weekend. I had asked her where we were going and she had said it was a surprise and I told her if I was driving it wouldn't be a surprise and she told me to just take a certain highway and I spoiled it all by guessing

Galena. LBH told me it would still be a surprise and I told her we're spending a weekend in Galena at a bed and breakfast and the only surprise would be which bed and breakfast and she was very pissed off by my deductions but come on you can't fool me. Had she been driving the weekend would have been a surprise although I would have known eventually and maybe would have bitten my tongue but I just can't do that. That weekend was further ruined by our breaking of the vintage bed when we had sex the first night and I had to cough up some extra money for that and well everything kind of went downhill although we were pretty much at the foot of the hill by then. And we didn't like the other people staying at the bed and breakfast and the television room smelled like cigarettes. I told LBH then and I still believe it to be true that it was very nice of her to spend her money on me like that and I didn't deserve it and she said You're right you don't but I needed to get out of the rotten city. So there's that story.

We wait in the car looking at the nothing and I think about saying, What a waste of time, but I keep my mouth shut as I'm remembering the way I don't bite my tongue. The possibly foreign couple doesn't move an inch but their little son or daughter is having a great time running around their nice economy car. LBH looks at them and says I hope they can control that kid. LBH and I have let enough minutes pass and get out of the car and I remember to take the keys. We mosey which is the only way to describe how we are moving. Oh we are great moseyers in the city in the country wherever we mosey. I mosey and nod to the possibly Asian couple and they smile and nod in return. The child stops when it sees us and holds up a model airplane and LBH says Oh I see and we still have no idea if it is a boy or a girl or a very small adult with really good skin.

It is very easy to describe nothing to you and I am going to do it. The nothing extends as far as the eye can see. Now when I say nothing it is not a void, I mean no there is earth of a dirt-like quality and only dirt. No fences no grasses no mounds no abandoned farm equipment no graves no signs no furrows. Powdery brown crumbly dry dirty dirt. Look as far as you like as far as you can and the only other thing you see is the sky and the sky is doing nothing. No clouds but the blurry sun is to our left so we must be facing north because it is the afternoon and that's all there is to describe. I fish my wallet out and look inside and find nothing but twenties and I tell LBH this and she tells me Ask for change you're not sticking me with the tab for this besides I've got nothing on me.

The child zooms around the economy car again making airplane noises and I say to the couple Hello and they nod again and LBH looks the other way. I say to the couple Cute kid is it a boy or girl and they nod and smile. I nod and smile. LBH spits. She is the only woman I know who spits. She used to be a smoker and she continues to be a very dedicated drinker.

A door on the side of the tour bureau opens and a not unattractive blonde woman in jeans t-shirt ratty fur coat and boots emerges.

"Afternoon, "she says. "If you'll line up on my left, please."

LBH and I line up on her left and let the silent couple stand in front of us because they were here first. The woman in the fur coat holds out her hand.

"Five dollars, please," she says. "I am your guide."

The man hands her three five-dollar bills and she gives him one bill back.

"Children are free," she says.

I hand her a twenty. She gives me the man's two fives.

"Isn't that interesting the way money makes its journey?" she asks. "One minute the money is warm inside a wallet and then it's in someone's hand and soon that someone passes it along to someone else and a new wallet for however long it's meant to be there. Isn't that interesting? Our money gets around more than we do."

All of us look at her.

"Let's begin," she says. "My name is Calixta. Photographs are allowed."

The man clears his throat at the child and the child trots up to him and stands still with the energy gone out of him or maybe just rebottled. Calixta tucks the twenty into her shirt pocket and runs a red nail polished hand through her hair.

"This way," she says.

She leads us beyond the cars and stops so we can see from a new vantage point and all we can see is her and a whole lot of nothing behind her.

"You have come to a point that is very similar to if not exactly like many other points in this fine country," she says. "You have been drawn here not by a desire to see nothing but by someone else's desire to make you desire to see nothing for a fee. In this era of everything and too much there can be a shack and a beautiful blonde in an old fur and there can be nothing. Here is the nothing."

She gestures to the nothing. LBH holds up her camera. Calixta notices this and poses as LBH takes a photograph and the man takes many photographs with his much nicer camera.

"You will say either to me or each other or to yourselves that what we are looking at is not exactly nothing it is something and this is true," Calixta says. "There is Earth and there is sky. Sky and Earth are something. But the sign was only so big and Nothing fits better than

Earth and Sky and essentially Nothing. For once you have mentally registered Earth and Sky you have nothing else. There is nothing interesting here. There is nothing happening. There is nothing that has been left behind. There is nothing that has been neglected. There is nothing different from the nothing on this side of the highway to the nothing on the other side of the highway other than on the other side of the highway nobody is charging you to take a tour of it. That is a fact and that concludes the factual part of the tour.

"This nothing has been here for quite a long time or so we assume. Our memories can only go back so far. It is possible that one hundred years ago a farm was here or a house but there is no memory of it and no record of such. It is possible that something once grew here. There is no memory of it and no record of it. It is possible that one hundred and fifty years ago a collection of people with horses and covered wagons rolled over this on their way to somewhere else. But there is no memory of this and no record of such. It is possible that two hundred years ago there were people native to this soil who actually lived and hunted and slept and loved and ate and died on this nothing. Imagine a thousand years prior to that. And a thousand years prior to that. And five thousand years prior to that. And ten thousand years prior to that. And fifty thousand years prior to that. And three hundred thousand years prior to that. And a million years prior to that. Imagine the birthday of this planet and then imagine this spot. It is possible that we are looking at the birth of this planet. And now if you'll follow me."

Calixta leads us into the nothing. It is soft and lacking any smell. The sounds of the highway become fainter. Calixta puts her pretty hands into the pockets of her fur. The woman takes the hand of her child. The child clutches the toy airplane. LBH takes my hand. Calixta stops and turns to us.

"If you look to your right you will see a continuation of the nothing but this is not to say that if you began walking in that direction that sooner or later you will happen upon something," she says. "In fact it is a certainty that sooner or later you will happen upon something. If you look to your left you will see more nothing and the same applies to this direction if you decide to start walking. Don't worry nobody is going to steal your cars. Behind you is the highway that makes escape possible. I point this out because in other times in automobileless times you could be standing here with nothing but your feet or perhaps a horse or perhaps a horse and wagon to take you away from this nothing. The highway is also what brings you here and here is what you want. If you want nothing, we have it. If nothing is what you want, there is plenty of it. You could even pass us and in the next fifty miles you will find a spot exactly like this. A spot full of nothing. At no charge. You are not fools. You are here and you paid because you are curious and I am here because I am curious about you and I need the money. There is only so much something. There can be continuous something but there is only so much of it that you take. You might be able to take it continuously and I know people like that. At any rate there is only so much nothing here and it is a contrast. If you do not think about these places do they exist? Certainly. They won't be existing for you but they will be existing for whoever is here when you are not thinking about them. And who is to say there is really nothing here? Look behind you."

We look behind us and see nothing but footprints. Smaller quicker footprints of the child. Two sets in tandem of the couple. LBH's starting far from mine and coming closer.

"And now look behind me," Calixta says.

We look behind her see footprints. Many of them. Overlapping. Small and large. A scampering. An aimlessness. A trodding.

"One year from now ten years from now twenty years from now a hundred thousand million years from now there will be no memory of us and even our tracks will be mashed down into nothing but that doesn't mean we are nothing," Calixta says. "It means we are something once we were something once."

LBH lets go of my hand.

"Thus concludes the non-factual part of the tour," Calixta says. "You are free to roam around and explore as long as you like. It gets dark around seven thirty."

She smiles and walks back to the hut. The child holds up the airplane and makes airplane sounds and runs further into the nothing and its parents follow it.

LBH and I don't move.

I think of that trip to Galena that was a surprise and wasn't a surprise and remember that even though we didn't much care for the people who were also at the bed and breakfast when we ate with them the next morning they all seemed friendly and they all assumed LBH and I were married. I remember how LBH picked at her cranberry muffin and smiled and blushed and told them we were brother and sister. I remember somebody dropping a fork because I know I know I know they all heard the bed being wrecked the night before. I remember this because it was so LBH.

LBH says I'm starving.

She and I walk back to the car, no, we mosey back to the car. There is no sign of Calixta as we approach the hut but there are other cars now and other people standing and waiting. A man asks us if we are the tour guides. I say, Yes but we're off duty the next guide will be along soon.

LBH says Wait and she turns around and takes one last picture of what we have seen and off in the distance moving further away are the tiny figures of the man and the woman and the running child and its toy held aloft.

LBH says Let's get out of here and I say Done and done and we drive away.

I say Where to and she says Surprise me.

The Cruel Weddings of
Ivy Lockton

They called them cruel weddings not because they felt Ivy was marrying for all the non-marrying reasons but because they found them difficult and hard and taxing and almost impossible to endure for a number of reasons. They felt this way because all of them were accustomed to soft, easy weddings of their older cousins or younger uncles or sisters or brothers. They knew they were the last of an era to attend weddings with smooth transitions from church to reception hall to honeymoon, weddings that were identical to the millions of weddings that happened before they were born. They knew Ivy Lockton shared this history of traditional unspecialness with them and they also knew Ivy Lockton wanted to rush away from that past as fast as her gartered legs could carry her.

They speculated Ivy Lockton was either a witch or had purchased a particularly accurate almanac for the years of her first three weddings as it rained the entirety of her first, snowed the second, and reached the apex of a heat wave on her third.

The belligerent rain on her first wedding lasted from dawn until midnight. It made roads slick or flooded, ended plans for outdoor photography, and cast a solemn, weepy pall over the occasion. They arrived with insufficient umbrellas and improvised slickers. They squished in their soaked dress socks and new hose. They damped their way from blazing church to nearly submerged banquet hall, uncomfortable and rubbery in their humid skin. They burgeoned with fresh mildew as they sat down to their prime ribs, trouts, or grilled vegetables. The first dance of the newlyweds was performed to the off-rhythms of a small band competing with rain drumming on the roof. They thought they and the world would never be dry again, although they and it were the very next day.

They have little if anything to say about the snow of the second wedding because many of them suffered because of it. It snowed from dawn to midnight, fat and impetuous snow that halted everyone's progress except the determined wedding party. Most of them by evening's end were forced to book overnight rooms at the hosting hotel secondary to disappeared roads and arctic conditions. Many of them could not get rooms and had to huddle around a roaring fire in the massive lobby's fireplace. Two of them were swallowed up by the weather when they insisted on braving their way home because the vehicle they owned was big and powerful and expensive and they were never seen again.

The heat wave that occurred during the third killed a further three of them directly and indirectly. This wedding had been held outside on the unshaded tee-off of a golf course. One of them dropped dead of sunstroke during the vows. One of them suffered heart failure while seated on the cool commode of the country club's men's room. One of them died the next day of unconfirmed causes but the rest of them knew it was because of the heat and humidity of the previous day.

Ivy Lockton continued. Her fourth wedding required all of them to travel to a distant state at their own expense. A quarter of them perished when the chartered plane they had booked to take them to the obscure mountain retreat smashed into an aggressive wall of rock.

The fifth wedding was a trifle easier on them. It resulted in no deaths but provoked an infestation of fleas in one of them and snapped ankles for two of them. The weather was clement the entire wedding, the food inventive but palatable, the gulf view tranquil, the surf sound hypnotizing, the dolphin sightings awe-inspiring, the vows unintelligible due to the roaring tide. That they were unaccustomed to walking on soft sand was their own problem as they had lived their lives prior to this in asphalted cities. They are not sure, but some of them are convinced that one of their number actually sank in the sand and never returned.

Ivy Lockton endured as she always had, marrying, divorcing, falling in love, naming the date, sending out the invitations, attending parties and showers thrown in her honor, tasting proposed menu items, selecting floral arrangements and centerpieces, auditioning bands, and confirming a steady trickle of gifts, dresses of white satin, and avowals of loving and honoring and obeying.

They began to suspect that Ivy Lockton's perpetual weddings were her way of winnowing her mass of friends down to the truest and heartiest and lovingest. They felt this because it was a cold and sinister feeling they felt whenever a thick pastel envelope slid through their mail slots. They noticed that fewer and fewer of their original set attended the weddings while their number stayed the same because Ivy Lockton was constantly making new friends and acquaintances. Yet they continued to RSVP, bracing themselves for hardships ahead.

They did this because they knew Ivy Lockton was Ivy Lockton as she always had been and was likely always to be and because they had a fascination for her and whatever could or would happen when next she brought them together in fancy dress. They found the wedding registries and ordered the stainless steel toasters and crystal cocktail shakers and turquoise place settings. They dry-cleaned their suits and bought new dresses. They hired babysitters and made sure their last wills and testaments were in order and checked to see if their insurance policies were paid up. They filled their wallets and clutches with embossed cards bearing the contact information of their next of kin.

They began small clubs to honor those of them who had not survived the weddings and to celebrate those of them who had. They met monthly and dined and drank and swapped stories and listened to lectures on the hazards of the world. The toasted the perished over end-of-evening brandies and fell into recollective silence.

The invitations continued. The sixth, the seventh. The eighth, the ninth.

They travelled to the edge of nowhere for Ivy Lockton's tenth. They checked into the sole hotel in this rim of obscurity, each of them arguing with the pimpled clerks who told them their reservations were for the day before. They stepped around gray puddles in the warped bathrooms, wrinkled their noses at decades-old cigarette smoke woven into the scratchy, gold coverlets, were elbowed aside by an exuberant high school baseball team rushing to the pool and causing a shortage in towels, and hoped Ivy Lockton's tenth would be her last.

They piled into overly air-conditioned charter buses and crawled deep into uncharted woods, inching along a narrow dirt path. Eager trees swiped against their bus windows. They did not talk amongst themselves. They watched civilization regress to nothing as they inched past neglected homes fronted by shirtless, bloated, grilling men and saggy, drinking women who watched them pass with yellow eyes. The homes gave way to trailers, then cabins, then shacks. Ancient foliage pressed in on them. The sun was engulfed by a high canopy of lowering trees. They pressed on in their heavy machines, creeping to some shadowy central retreat where Ivy Lockton waited with her latest groom.

They arrived. They drank murky liquors from huge spigoted glass urns. They were eaten alive by mosquitoes. They filled up on slushy ethnic food of unclear origin served from great heated pans. They didn't dare dance.

Ivy Lockton thanked them all for coming as she always did. She told them the ceremony would happen as soon as night fell, after the food and booze and insect repellant and music. Ivy Lockton then spent many minutes with each of them, old friends and new, calling herself the luckiest woman in the world for being blessed with so many good and supportive and solid and game people who were always prepared to follow her through all brands of weather and all stripes of terrain to celebrate her newest bout of fresh happiness.

They felt the darkness come. Ivy Lockton instructed them to follow her down a minimally marked trail that supposedly wound down to the water or a little distance from it. The more sober of them were given torches to light the way. They went, holding onto each other, down through the black vegetation and hidden animals. They crowded around a circular clearing in the density, a clearing not clearly made by man or nature. Someone quoted a stiff passage from an ancestral tome. Someone dipped a hollowed gourd into a murky liquid. They were instructed to face one direction, then another, then another until all points of the compass were honored and they were thoroughly confused.

A guitar played.

They could barely see one another.

They were packed together, trying to focus on the inky whiteness of Ivy Lockton, who smiled by torchlight and performed a short, slow dance with feathers.

They lost track of where they were and who they were. They were filled with thoughts of love or what it means to be in love or show love or promise love or if their homes and cars were locked and safe and unmolested. They felt sleepy and lulled and aware of their necks, or rather the weight of their heads as they sat on their necks. They heard music, smelled fire, wondered where the dog had come from.

They huddled together, closer than they ever had, arm seeking arm, chin finding shoulder, palm grasping hip. They sensed something was finally going to happen to them, something once and for all, something liberating for Ivy Lockton, dear Ivy Lockton, gorgeous Ivy Lockton, loving Ivy Lockton, blurry Ivy Lockton, friendly Ivy Lockton, always Ivy Lockton.

The Unreturned

Pleth went out looking for Gullenden and found him. Pleth was surprised by his success and became cocky. He told Jurnzen he would go out and look for all that were missing. "Call in Vashik and Frederlend and Kife and that little guy you didn't really trust but had to send out," Pleth said. "I will handle everything."

Pleth went out. While he was gone, they asked Gullenden why he had been missing. "I am too tired to go into it," he said, and they left him alone.

Pleth went out to the wooded area first because that was where he had found Gullenden, that was where he had felt his first surge of canniness. He carried the List of Unreturned, two meat paste sandwiches wrapped in wax paper, and a flask of his special brandy. He stepped on crisp leaves and damp dirt. He bathed in the morning quiet of the trees thrusting up from the world. He moved from sunbeam to sunbeam.

He found no one. He returned.

Gullenden said, "Do you want help?" Pleth denied help. "You needed no help becoming lost, did you?" he said, but Gullenden said he hadn't been lost at all. The others listened to them go at it. An excerpt from the minutes:

PLETH: You were lost because I found you.

GULLENDEN: You found me because I was where I was at the exact same time you were where I was.

PLETH: You make it sound like I did nothing more than find a rock or a pond or a tree. I did much more. Trees and rocks don't move, unless the former is being cut down and the latter is being thrown. As for ponds...

GULLENDEN: Listen, just because you say you found me doesn't mean you can find everybody and anything. You're skewing the language to make it mean more than it actually means.

PLETH: Ten bucks says if you went somewhere again and didn't return, I'd find you.

GULLENDEN: You're on, jackass.

Gullenden went somewhere and did not return. Pleth added his name to the List of Unreturned again and went out, this time into the city. He did not find him.

Nor did he find Shilker, Nish, Colmbrek, Devidovich, Krelp, or Telebatt. He returned and they had a good talking to him. He listened to all they said and, at a few minutes past midnight, handed over the List. They thanked him and went out.

Pleth went home. Gullenden was waiting for him.

"Ah," Pleth said, "I've found you." Gullenden told him he hadn't, but Pleth insisted. He had returned to his home and found Gullenden there, which means he found Gullenden. Gullenden shook him by the shoulders. "You weren't looking for me," he said. "You technically can't find me if you haven't been looking for me. That's ten bucks you owe me."

Pleth said, "Do mean to tell me that the only way someone can be found is if someone else is looking for them?" Gullenden said he wasn't saying anything of the kind, but if that's the way Pleth chose to interpret it, sure. "Now hand over the ten bucks," he said. Pleth resisted. "You tricked me," he said. "You were here all along, somewhere you knew I'd eventually find you." Gullenden said he knew nothing of the sort, because he had no assurance that once Pleth went out that he, too, might wind up being one of the unreturned. "If that's the case," Pleth said, "how long would you have waited here for me?" Gullenden said, "Long enough," and went out.

Pleth went to the bathroom and sat and thought. So many of them had gone out and not come back. So many of them still around were spending so much time looking for them. In light of Gullenden's words, it occurred to Pleth that their list was inaccurate; it was not a List of Unreturned but a List of Undiscovered. He wanted to tell Gullenden about his discovery, but feared Gullenden would put him to another test and get another ten bucks off of him.

Pleth went about his life for a few days and thought about the many of them who had become undiscovered. He mentioned his thoughts to Jurnzen, who said, "Explain." Pleth said, "If you want to be found, you will be found. If you want to remain undiscovered, you will remain undiscovered." He pointed to a copy of the List and said, "How do we know if those of us currently on the List are on the List because they want to be on the List and nowhere else?" Jurnzen brought up the phenomenon of Gullenden and added, "Does that mean Gullenden wanted to be found or returned or discovered or however you want to put it?"

Pleth said, "Yes."

And Gullenden went away again and eventually became unreturned. This time, his name was not added to the List. Jurnzen did not understand. "What is he doing," he said, "the old Boy Who

Cried Wolf routine?" Pleth shrugged. He offered to go out looking for him. Jurnzen said, "Up to you."

Pleth learned that the others who had gone out with copies of the List had been having no success in finding the other unreturned; in fact, a small number of those who had gone out became unreturned themselves, and the List grew instead of shrank. At that point, those remaining turned to Pleth and noted that thus far he had been the only one to find anyone, and would he go out again?

Pleth went out again but did not take the List with him. He did not take any sandwiches or brandy. He tipped his hat to those behind him and said, "I'll see what I find," and they said, "Don't you mean you'll see *who* you will find?" and Pleth said, "I mean what I say," and that was all he said.

Billy, Elaborated

First the hands stretch and crack into claws. Then the feet burst the Adidas. Next the skin hardens and turns the color of ancient seawater.

Someone calls him for the second time. Lunch.

The mouth shoots forward and sprouts ferocity. The head, rock-like and boulder-shaped, bumps the ceiling, which gives. The head punches through the rafters, thick hide and girder bones against tindery wood. They don't build 'em like they used to.

Another call. Lunch.

Indeed it is, but grilled cheese and tomato soup ain't gonna cut it anymore.

"Oh, Billy's fine, I guess."

"How'd it go at his school?"

"The usual. We had a little talk with the principal. He acted like he knows Billy personally, but he doesn't. There's like eight hundred kids in that school, they only start paying attention to you when you hit 7th or 8th grade."

"Well what did he say?"

"Who?"

"The principal."

"Nothing we haven't heard before. He's concerned about this and that, we should look into this and that, have we tried this and that, he recommends blah blah blah…"

"How'd he take it?"

"Who?"

"Billy."

"How d'you think he took it?"

"Not in the same way, I hope."

"Well, unfortunately we made the mistake of getting another cat."

"Jesus."

A mighty tail sprouts faster than a freight train across a Kansas prairie. The room comes apart, walls of sugar wafers. The house splinters and powders around him. Up, now, and out. Toenails are talons, big and lethal as plows, digging deep trenches in the yard, mangling the swing set, obliterating the garage, burying the roses and squash and the St. Francis birdbath.

Up, up, and out. Power lines snap with a helpless buzz. The 3200 block of Sunnyside is going, going, gone. There will be no more calls to lunch, guaranteed.

Mrs. Rassel will not ring the bell anymore because she knows it can be heard and those who aren't there are deliberately ignoring her so she tells those assembled to wait and she rounds the corner and sees one boy kicking another. The boy being kicked is on the ground, on his side, trying to wheeze a squeal. The boy doing the kicking is taking a great interest in his task. He has braced himself against the school and looks down at his victim. Mrs. Rassel screams. The kicker stops, buttons his coat, and goes inside.

What an immense feeling of enormity. What a liberating sensation of sheer power and strength. The impressions of everyone else are now of no importance. Look at them flee.

The ground is a magnet. Gravity is a selfish lover. Certainly the movements are slow; naturally the effort to take one step or raise one arm will be labored. Like a swimmer walking through water. There is a certain kind of elegance to this, this putting of the impressive, terrifying body in motion. There must be economy now, economy of thought in terms of where to go and what to do and how soon to do both. But of course there is only one action. Shift the weight a little to the right and press on. It can be seen from here. The school.

"Put the kid in sandals, he'll think twice about kicking anybody."

"That's not a solution."

"It's a damn good solution."

"It's not a solution that's going to help the situation."

"Anybody ask if the other kid deserved it?"

"Three broken ribs and possible internal bleeding?"

"I'm asking if the kid deserved it."

"I can't imagine what any little boy could do to deserve that."

"Hey, one thing leads to another, you know?"

"Perhaps your wife could join the conversation."

"She's, uh, she's away for a little while."

Who lives in these houses is irrelevant. They are in the way. Not even in the way, hardly obstacles. They are in the path. This is like walking through a field of clover. Who is driving that bus, police car, Toyota—doesn't matter. You people are in the wrong place at the wrong time. Hope you're at peace with your Lord.

Fire. Is there fire? A little cough—nothing. There has to be fire. Something must trigger it. A burp. A hissing. A way of opening the mouth. Try all three. Nothing. Ah, nuts. Had the heart set on a little fire.

In summary, the subject is otherwise a friendly and talkative individual, surprisingly forthcoming and candid for one so young. One does not have the feeling that something is "off." The home situation, certainly, could be improved, but that is not a topic for this report. The subject may not be apologetic, but neither is there bitterness or malevolence. I am reticent to recommend too stringent a discipline. While the case certainly bears watching, I think aggressive monitoring would only stunt the subject's social development at this time. I recommend token damages be awarded the owner of the deceased cat and reimbursement for fuel expended in the initiation of what the subject has called "the experiment," but otherwise I strongly regard this as an isolated incident that should be handled with minimal follow-up.

The slight demerit of this long-awaited and much-desired transformation is the thought that all retribution will be swift, swifter than required. One drop of the enormous foot, one pound of the powerful fist, and the destruction is complete. The moment will not be savored. The question, too, is what to do with oneself after the objective is met? Similar attacks following the first will soon become boring, redundant. Will the goal, then, be to terrorize rather than annihilate? If only the damn fire-breathing feature would work. Shouldn't it work?

Are those jet planes?

The manager looks at the application, sees something unusual where something unusual should not be, and doesn't know whether to laugh or be cautious. He casts another glance at the applicant, who sits comfortably but not familiarly in the chair opposite the desk. The applicant's expression is hard to read: calm? Bemusement? Provocation? The manager returns his concentration to the application. Everything else is normal; too normal. A not impressive applicant, but none are. The rare exceptions do not apply for the job in question. The manager finds the remark that made him take pause, reads it again, and takes up a pencil, which he taps on the desk.

"Quite a sense of humor," he says.

"Me?"

"Yeah. Ha. 'Briefly became fire-breathing monster at age ten.' That's a new one on me."

"Everybody says that."

Troubled by the answer, the manager stops tapping the pencil. A good look at the applicant. "Where did you grow up?" he asks.

"It isn't there anymore."

The manager takes the application in both hands, hands he notices are now slightly damp. All he wants to do is go home at the end of the day, convince his wife to have sex with him one more time, save enough money to go on a big vacation somewhere someday, be popular with his superiors, earn more than the usual merit increase at the end of the fiscal year, need to have no more bridge work, keep most of his hair, have enough luck with his investments to retire early, and not get cancer.

"Well," he says to the applicant, "I'd like to start you in sales."

The original school burned to the ground in 1896, one year after it was built. The earth was salted and a new building was built, this time of stone, but it, too, burned to the ground in 1926. The present building was built in 1926 or 1928. No one, currently, is certain. The cornerstone says 1928, but didn't we hear a story once that the cornerstone was miscarved yet the school board laid it anyway? And how could someone miscarve a cornerstone? How could you not get to a certain point without realizing the error? And who in their right mind would think that the order asked for a cornerstone dated two years in the future? Regardless, where did the kids go to school between 1926 and 1928?

The school remained unchanged until 1984, when new windows were installed, the band room converted into a science lab, and the asbestos tiling pulled out and replaced. Many other changes were made, most of them internally. The Multipurpose Room became the Computer Lab. The wooden bleachers in the gym were replaced with aluminum. The framed class photos dating back to 1926 or 1928 were removed from where they hung near the ceiling along the main corridor by the principal's office and stored in what used to be the K–6 Music Room. The handsomely carved water fountains were replaced by boxy, humming, gunmetal water fountains.

The playground was resurfaced in 1997. All of the dangerous playground equipment was removed and replaced by nothing.

Later, when the school was crushed, it was not rebuilt. There was nobody left to rebuild it.

"I don't know what's going on with you, but you're to go to your room and stay in your room until we say you can come out. We'll bring a TV up after you've done your homework. You can use the old Sony that's on the porch. There are old movies on Channel 9. If you don't like it, tough.

"I'm sorry. We don't know what else to do. What you did to that little girl and then all those cars and now this thing at the Jewel, well...what else can we do? Where did this come from? You're such a sweet boy, you're so smart. We know you're smart. We have the test scores. And your teachers like you. Everyone likes you. But what is this?

"Is it us? It can't be us. This is why it hurts us, makes us so sad to have to treat you like this. For now. Okay? Okay?"

Mission accomplished, and I now understand that the savoring will happen now, now that it's over. I know it's over because the upsurge of release, of meaning, brought the fire. The savoring comes now, now that I can keep this day in my mind, in my memory. Here is the grand gesture: a turning away, slowly. That's it. Not the deed itself but the walking away from the dead. I will make my way to a body of water. Yes, I need to be cooled. No one is going to stop me. Oh, sure, they will try to stop me, or think they know how to stop me, but their efforts will be, at best, mere entertainment. Here I go.

Leaving. Leaving ruin behind me. Not the ruin I caused, but the ruin that was already there. This is what I'll say if ever they ask me. The ruin was already there, and that is the beauty of Billy, he knows when to clear the ruin away. Oh, yes.

Oh, yes.

How to Handle
the Educated

How to handle the educated.

Don't invite them over.

Unless you have to. I have to because we're related to them. That is, the wife invites them over. Must remember to refer to the wife as Bonnie because calling her the wife might make me seem something not cool. Douche-like.

Going back.

How to handle the educated.

She's okay but he's a tool. She's okay because when he's talking nobody gets a word in edgewise. She's okay in a way because she's the sister-in-law. I think I can get away with just calling her the sister-in-law even though her name's Janet. It's not like we're on intimate (God forbid!) terms. Anyway, she's okay even though she's just like him only he always gets the jump on the conversation which is never a conversation with him it's more like a lecture. "You know, the interesting thing about that," that's how it always starts with him, and he's good to go, launching into an oral epic about something that, as it turns out, isn't interesting at all and that's why I drink more. You see, you drink less when your mouth is engaged in something other than drinking, like talking, like when you have a conversation, not when you're listening to some windbag bloviate (I picked that word up somewhere, I forget). Then your mouth's got nothing to do but drink and so you drink faster, which allows you to drink more.

Drinking more is one way to handle the educated. Sort of. The trouble with drinking more (I'm talking alcohol here, you're safe with soda pop) is that the alcohol loosens up the mouth or it loosens up the brain, and so your brain is devising all these smart things to say to shut up whoever's lecturing you about some shit's got nothing to do with anything and so when your brain is loosened it all comes spilling out. And then the evening ends early and everyone's looking at you like you were a douche. Going back.

How to handle the educated. She's okay when she's not talking because he is talking but there are times when the two of them get going together and it's like you're getting nails driven into your skull. They get going on their glass tables and their tapestries and all the things their cars do and the interesting points brought up in so-and-so's latest article on whatever and it's pound, pound, pound the nails go in. They want to know what you've been reading lately and the answer is nothing only you don't say nothing you say, A little of this a little of that, some really interesting shit or you say, I've been fishing around for something good to read, what'd you say the name of that journal was?

How to handle the educated. Know something they don't know. They often don't know anything about sports. I knew a guy once only knew about the Revolutionary War it was like he lived through it and anything'd get him going about some battle or some document and Jesus we'd all be asleep in no time. So one way I'm thinking is to know something they don't know and know everything about it. I said sports but other things are good. Bonnie knows gardening and she's up on the TV programs. I know baseball and basketball and football and hockey and golf and model trains. The difficulty is sliding all this stuff naturally into a conversation when you're with somebody who doesn't know shit about any of it. How 'bout them Cubs? out of nowhere often doesn't cut the mustard. Going on/back.

How to handle the educated. She's okay if she's good looking.

The wife breaking in here (Bonnie—hello). Jim started this because he's resentful or because he's envious, so I'm sorry. Jim's a lot of fun but not when they're around. Now the thing is we don't see Janet and Gifford all that often but they're close (they live close by) and she's my sister and she's a rotten cook, she doesn't cook much. We're so proud of her. I mean my family is so proud of her. She's done so much. I've got copies of the photos, four of them, all in the living room on the whatnot shelves, all of them with her in cap and gown, graduating from somewhere. You visit their apartment and you see her diplomas, they're framed, they're in her study. Just think, to have a study, a room in your house or your apartment or wherever that's called a Study. Because you study there. I know she studies, she always has, she's still studying, even though she's not in school anymore, she studies, she and Gifford study. I imagine it's nice and quiet in their apartment, he in his study and she in hers, maybe there's classical music going. I know they listen to classical music, the two times they've had us over there's been classical music playing, softly, you know the kind, the kind that sounds like you're in a museum or in one of those programs on PBS where they're all having tea in the drawing room and wearing coats and vests and dresses.

I got off track there, I was apologizing for Jim's attitude, even though he's the one who started this, he just gets so angry. He's envious. Jim isn't dumb, he's just full of envy, maybe he thinks he should've learned more although I think he knows a lot. He knows more than me and he makes a hell of a sandwich. Anyway, I'm going to warn you now that Jim's way of handling the educated is not necessarily "The Way" of handling the educated but they do need to be handled.

How to handle the educated. First, shut them up fast.

Nope, I'm wrong, that's not first. First, study them. Your natural reaction will be to get them out of the house as fast as possible but hang on a little and get to know your prey. No, not your prey, your enemy. No, they're not really your enemy either. They're something. Look, it's not my fault. I had a problem up until fifth grade and they thought it was because I couldn't see the blackboard clearly and so I got glasses and they didn't help my performance any. Then they said I was bored and needed to be challenged but that wasn't it either because when I was challenged I was bewildered and I don't remember half the shit I sat through. I spent three years in Algebra in high school. Everybody else was moving on to Calculus but by my senior year I was stuck in the class with the jocks.

I was a jock sort of. I say sort of because the guys in track weren't really considered jocks, we just ran. So we were fit but it's a quiet sport. I wasn't on the football team. But I had to take classes with those meatheads. A lot of those guys now are selling real estate or teaching gym at grade schools.

Back to the educated. Study them. Really listen. They're smart about a bunch of things but you only really need to latch on to just one thing like music or painting or 17th Century modes of whatever. Latch onto that one thing and then go away and read a bunch of things about that one thing and the next time they're over you can chime in. Trust me, they'll shut up. And here's why.

He's a douche, as I've said. He loves to get all academic whenever we're over, the rare times they decide to host, and they've got paintings all over their apartment, just paintings, but they've got them lit from above in special lights and they climate control the rooms. So he likes to drag me around the place looking at the paintings and he always asks what do I think and I don't know what to say, they're all a little messy. So this one last time we were over he and I stood in front of this one painting and he went on and on about the guy who painted it and what it's meant to represent and I wanted to punch him.

So later I took an afternoon and went to our local library (which is real nice now they've redone it, it's a new building and everything, I hadn't been in there since I was a kid, I mean been in the old library that used to be where the new one is) and looked up this painter and the painting and I read a bunch of things about it and the next time we're over and he's holding forth I made a comment about the painting, I said, That's very true, but Owenton, in his latest critical essay, found evidence that links this particular piece with the Shepley-Hill movement of the late 1950s, and when you consider it in that light, it makes more sense. That shut him up good.

Because he's the kind of guy who's not happy being educated, he's got to lord it over the rest of us. Ten bucks says when he's with his other educated friends he comes off as a real dope. I'll bet he's the runt of the litter. I'll bet he's like a mental midget compared to the kinds of people he normally hangs around. So one way to handle the educated is to get them to shut up by making them fear you for the moment and they'll back off until the next time.

Another way to handle the educated is to have a baby.

Bonnie here. I just want to point out that it's unfair of Jim to bring up the baby thing. Janet and Gifford have always wanted a child but Janet can't have one. She didn't find that out until she was older. They spent a while having sex and then they got married so they were a little older then and then when they were trying in earnest and found nothing was working they figured it was either Janet or Gifford who was at fault and it turned out to be Janet. So she can't have kids. If she had a kid it'd be a miracle, and I just want to say here that my husband is very mean to bring this up as a way to shut them up.

My sister and I are not in competition. I just want to say that. There was never any race to see who'd be first to reproduce. Never. Jim and I just didn't have kids until now because I've been on the pill. When he asked me to go off the pill I said okay and it was business as usual. He didn't say to me then, Let's have a kid so we can be better than that sister of yours and her douchebag husband. No, I just want to say that for all his coarser behavior he didn't say that. We're not better than they are. But I know in some way this, this baby makes us an authority on something they're not an authority on.

We're going to name him Dustin because that's a nice name.

How to handle the educated. First, define what you mean by educated. Educated is someone who's been to school enough to know how to read and write and do arithmetic but also someone who's read a few good books and looked at some paintings and also maybe learned a second language like Mexican or maybe took a course in Religion or Comparative Something-or-other. Educated, really, is someone who is educated and makes a point of showing everybody else he or she has been educated.

There are things you know you just pick up. Like for instance how you shouldn't eat pizza or soup on a day you're wearing a new white dress shirt. Or how you should save your pocket change in a jar you keep in the kitchen and then use it on the few times you take a trip that requires the use of a tollway and then you always have exact change. Or how to hang pictures on the wall so they don't fall off it.

So in that way I'm educated, and a lot more, too.

The wife and I are going to name the kid Frank after my father even though she thinks right now we're going to call him Dustin. Dustin Hoffman is a short actor. Frank is a solid name.

So maybe it's not a question of handling or maybe it is. I don't know. You come up against a wall and common sense says you should look to your right or your left or above you to find a way around it or over it, you just shouldn't keep coming up against that wall. Even if it's a really wide wall.

And with luck this has been a big help to you.

Lasting

Matthias tells me that with all the money I spent on porn last week I could have bought something lasting. "Who says I bought any porn last week, or ever?" I ask.

"I says. $76.30 worth."

"And how did you come by this information?"

"I'm not accusing you of anything, I just made an observation."

"It was one of those snide observations you so often make."

"I don't do anything of the sort."

"Can't a guy buy a little porn every now and then?"

"Buy all you like. I just made the comment because you're always complaining about this cheap furniture and how you need new clothes and how you'd love to buy a really nice pair of shoes, the kind that doesn't fall apart after six months."

"You still haven't explained how you know of my expenditures."

"The delivery box with the bill inside is still in the trash."

"And why, may I ask, were you going through my garbage?"

"I wasn't going through it, I was throwing something out."

"What were you throwing out?"

"The half a grapefruit you didn't finish at breakfast."

"You don't have to clean up after me."

"You're just going to let things rot?"

"I'd get to it eventually, I always do. I'm not exactly wading through filth here, you know."

"Me throwing out the grapefruit was not meant to be a commentary on what a slob you are."

"But that remark was, right?"

"No."

"For all you know, I wasn't even done with the grapefruit yet."

"What were you going to eat, the peel?"

"Maybe I hadn't gotten out all the juice yet."

"It was as hard as a bowl. For all I know that was grapefruit from yesterday."

"Monday, actually."

"Okay, now you can interpret my throwing out of the grapefruit as a commentary on what a slob you are."

"I'm not a slob. I'm forgetful."

"How could you forget something like that? It was sitting in the middle of the dining room table."

"Just don't go through my trash."

"I already told you I wasn't going through your trash."

"What I mean is, if you have to throw something out, if you absolutely can't live another second on this planet without cleaning up after me, then just put whatever it is in the garbage and walk away. Don't go snooping."

"I wasn't snooping. You'd put the box in there and it didn't really fit, so I took it out, folded it up to make it smaller, and that's when the shipping thing, the shipping statement fell out."

"And you had to look at it."

"I didn't have to look at it, but I did."

"So you were snooping."

"I wasn't snooping, I was reading. You see words, you read. You can't help it if you know the language. You pass a guy reading the paper, your eye catches the headline, you read it."

"When's the last time you, me, or anybody passed a guy reading a newspaper?"

"I just chose a random illustration of my point."

"Your point being?"

"That I wasn't snooping, I was just reading, casually, as one reads things in passing because one can't help it."

"And it bothered you."

"I told you, it doesn't bother me that you bought $76.30 worth of pornography. Buy all the pornography you like. Join a Porn-of-the-Month Club. Buy your own warehouse."

"It does bother you, else you wouldn't have memorized the exact amount."

"The what?"

"That's twice now you quoted the exact amount of my purchase."

"And that means I'm bothered by your purchase?"

"You could've been approximate, you could've said $75 worth, or you could've just left the total out altogether, if all you were doing was making a casual, misinterpreted as snide, offhand, not caring comment."

"I saw $76.30 and so I said $76.30. I didn't memorize anything."

"But you brought it up."

"$76.30 is a lot of money."

"Hey, it could've been more, but the titles I picked up were on sale and I had an extra 15% discount by using the promotion code in the email."

"I congratulate you on your thrift. How many of these money-saving emails from porn outfits do you get?"

"That's another topic entirely."

"Fine, I don't really care."

"It's not like I buy the stuff every day."

"I don't even know why you need it in the first place."

"Meaning what?"

"Our sex life is pretty good, if you ask me."

"You won't hear me complaining."

"But somehow you feel the need to spend $76.30 on two pornographic DVDs."

"What's with all the talk of need? I never said I needed any of it. I just ordered the damn things. On a whim. And again with the quoting of the exact amount!"

"May I see them?"

"See what?"

"Your purchases."

"You know, I've just figured out your purpose here today. You're deliberately trying to back me into some kind of corner."

"What are you talking about?"

"You are. I don't know what your game is, but I feel like I'm being hassled. What do I need to buy porn for? I don't. But now and then I become intrigued, you know? Maybe on some basic level I want to see what younger guys are doing. I'm of a certain age, as my mother used to say of my father, and whereas you may be completely comfortable with the way you look and the way you're getting older and our sex life and all that, I might still be insecure, I might be a little curious."

"So you're telling me you buy the stuff for educational purposes."

"As in do I need to see it so I can figure out what to do with you when we're both in our friskier modes? Do you think I need education in that realm?"

"I am not impugning your ability to arouse and surprise me, nor am I questioning your occasional inventiveness. I am just saying that perhaps instead of spending all this money—and please note that I did not refer to the exact amount this time—instead of spending all this money on pornography involving 18-year-old Latino thugs..."

"So you looked at the titles!"

"I saw the total; the titles were just to the left. In fact, I saw the titles first, because I read left to right, just like everybody I know."

"All right, enough with the lecture on the reading habits of human beings. Just tell me the truth: you think less of me because I bought the stuff this one lousy time."

Matthias laughs at me then, one of those incredulous, high-pitched laughs, and goes down the hall to the spare bedroom. I follow him. "Where are you going?" I ask, my palms suddenly sweaty.

He opens the doors on the bottom of the bookcase, exposing a row of Louis L'Amour novels, dustjackets facing front. One falls over, exposing a stack of DVDs and VHS tapes. "One lousy time, huh?" he asks. "What about all these other lousy times?"

"Why were you snooping in there?"

"I wasn't snooping."

"You keep saying you're not a snoop but somehow you keep finding all this secret stuff."

"What gets me is why you think you have to hide it!"

"Are you kidding? I have company over, maybe my folks are visiting and they're using this room, do you think I want them coming across this stuff? Do you think it should be on the shelf with the other stuff, filed in alphabetical order? *Schindler's Fist* preceding *Schindler's List?*"

"You don't actually have one called *Schindler's Fist*, do you?"

"No, but I've seen it advertised."

"Maybe what I mean is I don't know why you think you have to keep this collection a secret from me."

"I'd hardly call it a collection."

"It's certainly more than a stash. There are videotapes in here going back to 1986! Were you collecting this stuff in junior high?"

"No, those were clearance tapes from when the mom and pop video store near where I used to live started going digital."

"Why have you kept them?"

"Because."

"Brilliant response."

"Look, I'll get rid of them all right now if it'll shut you up."

"Shut me up?"

"I meant make you happy."

"All right, all right, before I really flip my lid, let me just say that you're welcome to your porn. I'm not judging you. I've seen plenty of porn in my life, I'm no stranger to it. And I'm totally aware that everybody is different, not all of us think that porn is essentially a waste of time because it's essentially all the same and gets boring after like the first or second scene. Just because I outgrew it doesn't mean you had to outgrow it, too. What bothers me is you can't be open about it."

"What, was I supposed to announce on our first date that I have a small collection of porn?"

"It's not small."

"Whatever! Is that what I was supposed to say? And risk you turning out to be a prude? How you wouldn't go out with a guy who's hung onto his porn?"

"I can't answer for what you should've said when we started going out, as that was a hundred years ago, and obviously it doesn't matter all that much to me, as I've known about your stash for some time now and haven't said anything about it."

"And why not?"

"Because it's a touchy subject with you."

"It is not. I'm discussing it now."

"Sure, because you found out I was onto you."

"Onto me? You're using language now that reeks of some sort of covert investigation, like I'm a criminal. All that stuff is perfectly legal."

"You shouldn't have leapt all over me when I made that remark about spending the $76.30 last week. That's all."

"I'm just supposed to let you make remarks like that to me without saying anything? And what, exactly, is your idea of something lasting?"

"The furniture, the clothes, the shoes."

"None of that stuff is lasting. None of it lasts. Even if I did buy a $150 pair of shoes, they'd wear out, eventually. The clothes, too. The furniture maybe a little longer than the clothes and the shoes, but it, too, wouldn't last. What do you mean by something lasting?"

"I don't know. Forget I said anything."

"Too late. I keep these videos because at one time or another I find them or a moment within them especially hot or arousing and now and then I like to revisit those moments. I can't help it. I'm of a certain age and you should be grateful, not critical, that I've kept all of this stuff."

"Grateful?"

"Because my collection means that if I want to be satisfied in some other way that doesn't involve you, physically, I can turn to these videos and not to some other guy."

"That'd be fine if your tastes weren't all over the map."

He flips over the remaining novels and some of the videos come spilling out. "Black guys, Asian guys, skateboarders," he says, pointing, "dudes in leather, dudes in drag, dudes that might not be dudes…"

"Stop."

"You collect everything that isn't me."

"I had a rather limited range of personal experience before I met you."

"So what are you saying?"

"I'm saying that while you are very good at ignoring your fantasies, I ain't. But at least I'm not going out, behind your back, gathering experience based on my fantasies."

"Well, what do you want? A medal?"

I push him. He loses his balance and falls backwards. I apologize and ask him if he's hurt. "No," he says.

"Let me help you up."

"I can manage."

"I'll get rid of all this stuff, I promise."

"You don't have to. I know it's there, and you know I know it's there, so go on, enjoy, enjoy."

"I'm sorry I lost my temper."

"Yeah."

"I'm just not comfortable letting out my secrets."

"Oh? What other secrets do you have?"

"None."

"Really? You said secrets, which is plural. What else are you hiding from me?"

"Nothing."

"I'm supposed to believe you?"

"Look, I'm a boring person. I live my life and that's it. I have no secrets. This porn thing isn't really a secret, because if I really wanted the stuff to not be found then I would've done a better job at hiding it. I'd've kept them off site, in an oak chest buried in the yard, or in a safe deposit box, or at a friend's place. Do you see what I'm saying?"

"You're defensive. And not in the good way. And when you can't talk your way out of something, you get violent."

"Violent? You call a little push violent?"

"It was an act of aggression."

"And how often in the four years we've been together have I done that?"

"Never."

"See?"

"This only leads me to believe that there's something more about this collection of yours that you don't want me to know about."

"You're crazy."

"Am I?"

"Like what, for instance?"

"I have no idea. Perhaps you're into children or something, and there's a collection of child pornography hidden somewhere else. That this current collection so poorly masked by a row of Westerns—who stacks books face front? It just screams "hiding place"—this collection is actually a smokescreen. For all I know, you've got an even larger collection of heterosexual porn that reflects you're true tastes and preferences!"

"Now that's just stupid."

"No, it's all too believable."

"What straight man in his right mind would have a relationship with another man for one minute, let alone four years?"

"I don't know. You could be that sick. God knows what else I'm going to find."

"I don't like a snooper."

"That's because you've got something to hide."

"I don't."

"Oh? Why don't I just go through the garbage again and see what else I find?"

"So you admit it! You were going through my trash!"

"Then, I wasn't. Now, I will."

He makes a dash for the kitchen and I go after him. He nearly makes it, but I grab his arm and pull him sharply away. I hear something pop. He cries out in pain. "You've fucking dislocated my shoulder!" he yells. "You've dislocated my goddamn shoulder!"

I call him two days later, thinking he's had time to cool down. I ask him how he feels.

"Sore."

"At me?"

"Yes. And also my shoulder's sore."

"What can I do to make it up to you?"

"Nothing. Just leave me alone."

I call him again the next day. "I threw everything out," I say.

"Everything?"

"The DVDs, the videotapes, the whole shebang. Gone."

"Where?"

"In the trash. The dumpster."

"You idiot, kids go through the trash, you're going to leave all that stuff for kids to find?"

"What kids?"

"You live five blocks from the high school."

"I have never in the eight years I've been here seen anybody go through my trash."

"You could get arrested."

"For what?"

"For leaving explicit material somewhere that minors could get their hands on it."

"There's no coal mine around here."

"Minors as in the underaged, dunce."

"I know. I was trying to be funny."

"Well, you failed. Now go get that stuff out of the dumpster before you go to jail."

I do as he asks because I have no desire to go to jail. I also want to get on his good side again, but at the moment I hustle out to the alley I'm more concerned about cops knocking on my door at some future point with a passel of traumatized high schoolers in tow.

The dumpster is empty.

I conclude it was emptied by the garbage men even though it isn't my block's trash day, but it could be because Monday could have been some sort of holiday I hadn't been aware of and so everything got pushed back a day. I remember, however, that I'd upended my collection of porn into the dumpster over twenty-four hours ago, so for all I know the scavenging kids could have made off with the lot long before the dumpster was emptied.

I call Matthias but he doesn't answer.

He continues to not answer over the weekend.

I visit him. He answers the door. I say, "Ta-da!" and direct his gaze to my feet. "Well?" I ask.

"New shoes."

"Yup."

"Well, I hope they're made for walking. Goodbye."

His arm is in a sling.

"When do you get out of that thing?"

"Soon."

"I'll never forgive myself."

"You shouldn't."

"And yet I'm hoping you can forgive me."

"I'd rather not have to worry about what's going to happen next time I make some remark that doesn't agree with you."

"That was a once-in-a-lifetime accident. Honestly."

"But do you know? Do you know for sure?"

"Yes."

"I don't."

"Wait a minute. Four years, and that's it?"

"That's it."

"Can't we at least talk about it?"

"After the way the last conversation ended up? No thanks. Look, I'm not in any position to tell you what to do, but I can suggest that you don't bother me anymore. I won't be receptive, and I will call the cops."

He closes his door. I hear him lock it.

I go back to my place and throw out the day-old spaghetti sitting on the sideboard. I figure with nothing better to do it might be time to haul my bicycle out of my storage closet and take a spin around the neighborhood. I change clothes and head down to the basement. I take the bicycle out and see it either needs air in the tires or new tires altogether. I wheel it down the block to the gas station. I pass the mail carrier. She says hello, I say hello. She sifts through the stack of mail in her hand and gives me the few pieces for me she can find. She asks me if I'm taking advantage of the nicer weather. I tell her yes and how I need more exercise. She reaches into the mailbag and brings out a package. She hands it to me.

Loami

[Loami is a village in Sangamon County, Illinois, population 804 at the 2000 census. It was incorporated in 1875 and has a total area of 1.05 square miles.]

They sit at the kitchen table after dinner longer than usual. She says "Maybe we could get Jim Cloyd to drive us," and he says "He does us enough favors," and she says "He's always asking," and he says "That's taking advantage," and she says "He'd understand," and he says "It's a four hour drive, which means it's a five hour drive, maybe six, figuring in traffic and stopping somewhere for gas or something to eat or both," and she says "It doesn't hurt to ask," and he says "Then you do the asking, and if he says yes, fine, but both of us can't go," and she says "Why not?" and he says "He can't fit the three of us in his truck, and even if he says he can do you think any of us'd be comfortable hip-to-hip for six hours on the road with the heat the way it is?" and she says "Didn't think of that," and he says "And then you have to figure where we'd stay," and she says "With Frank, I suppose," and he says "Did he offer?" and she says "No, but that may be because it didn't come up, at least when I talked to him, did he say anything to you about it?" and he says "No," and she says "I wonder if he figures we wouldn't come anyway," and he says "That's what he figures, I'll bet, but it'd still have been nice of him to ask, to offer," and she says "If Jim says he'd drive us, we'd have to leave the day before, which is tomorrow, and we could be on the road again after and get home the next night," and he says "Jim can't do night driving," and she says "Who says?" and he says "He told me, once. I don't remember why. But it's true. You ever see him out driving around at night?" and she says "No, but I don't see anybody out driving around at night. Anyway, if that's the case then we'd have to stay another night, so it's only two nights we'd have to stay with Frank if we ask him and he says it's okay, and if not, that's only two nights we'd have to find a place," and he says "That's a lot of money," and she says "Not if we use our senior discount and stay at one of those little motor lodges or motels just outside the city. These dishes aren't going to wash themselves."

She gets up, takes the two plates to the sink, returns for the glasses, takes them to the sink, returns for the forks and knives, takes them to the sink, runs hot water, closes the drain, spritzes dishwashing liquid into the sink, waits. He says "We're forgetting Jim. He drives us, or one of us, he'll need a place to stay, too. And if Frank can't put us up, we'd have to pay for Jim's motel room, and his meals, too, not to mention paying him back for the gas, at least three tankfulls, the way I figure it, although why he'd say yes to any of it would be a mystery to me," and she says "He's a nice man," and he says "Carting you into Chatham once a week to do your shopping is one thing, but spending twelve hours round-trip with two old farts is another thing," and she says "He doesn't just take me shopping, he takes you and me to the doctor's, too," and he says "That's only twice a year," and she says "Knock wood."

She raps her knuckles on the cabinet above her and to her left. He says "What's that?" and she says, "I was knocking wood," and he says "Thought someone was at the door," and she says "No, it's me knocking wood, because I said 'knock wood,' so I knocked wood, and I'm surprised you could hear that with your back to me," and he says "Nothing wrong with my hearing," and she sets the dishes and glasses to dry, wipes the utensils, puts them away, lets the water out of the sink, dries her hands on a towel. She says "Do we have any of the Cherry Heering left?" and he says "What?" and she says "The cherry brandy," and he says "Cherry Heering isn't brandy, it's a liqueur," and she says "Do we have any of it left?" and he says "I don't know," and she says "Well, I could use a shot of it tonight," and he says "Let me see."

He goes into the dining room and opens the china cabinet. He moves aside the World's Fait salt and pepper shakers and reaches for a bottle partially hidden behind the smoked glass ham plate. He says "You got a good memory," and brings the bottle into the kitchen. She says "I remember because George made such a big deal about giving it to you that one Christmas, kept saying how you'd finally have something fancy in the house for guests," and he says "Yeah, and I remember now how he took the first shot out of the bottle," and she says "That was years ago, now I think about it. He's been dead twenty years," and he says "Twenty-two," and she says "I'll bet we haven't opened that bottle more than once. I wonder if it's still good?" and he says "This stuff doesn't go bad. Can't seem to get it open," and she says "Let me get those special liqueur glasses my Aunt Gladys gave me for a wedding present," and she goes into the dining room.

He says "Damn. Cork broke off," and she says "What?" and he says "Cork broke!" and she returns with the tiny glasses. She says "Poke it into the bottle," and he says "Then it'll be all corky," and she says "I'll strain it, it's no big deal." He pokes the broken cork into the bottle. She takes a strainer from a drawer and a Mason jar from a cabinet, places the one over the other, and pours the liqueur into the jar. She says "I just thought of something. Why not just ask Jim to drive us into Springfield, we could take a plane," and he says "That's worse," and she says "If it's the expense, I'm sure we have enough, " and he says "Yes, it's the expense, and I know you're going to tell me how cheap I am and that I shouldn't be concerned about the cost of everything, especially at a time like this, but let me remind you..." and she says "Okay, okay, don't let's go into this," and he says "Well, you start up with this and you make me feel ashamed of myself," and she says "I didn't start up with anything," and he says "And why didn't Frank offer to fly us in?" and she says "It never came up, and besides, I'm sure he's hurting too, now, I think he's been out of work," and he says "He didn't mention that to me," and she says "Well, why would he? There were plenty of things you never mentioned to your father-in-law," and he says "Why do you have to put it like that? Why don't you ever refer to him as your father?" and she says "Because I know who he is, I don't have to remind myself, I just say it that way to you to put it into perspective for you," and he says "What are you talking about? And what things didn't I mention to your father?" and she says "Never mind," and he says, "Oh, sure, you bring something up and then you say 'never mind' when I get hot about it," and she says "Listen, Frank has got his hands full with the arrangements, this is not a cheap time for him, I didn't expect him to offer to pay for a flight for us, and if he had, I'd've told him no," and he says "I can't remember the last time I was on an airplane," and she says "When we went to Fort Meyers that one time," and he says "That can't be. That was forty years ago," and she says "It wasn't as long as that. No, maybe it was. It was. Suzy was eight, so that makes it forty-two years ago," and he says "God," and she says "I think it's safe," and he says "What?" and she says "The brandy. I mean the liqueur."

He fills two glasses with the strained liqueur. She says "Not here, let's take it into the sitting room." They each take a glass and go into the sitting room. She says "I can never get used to summer. Dinner's over and it's still bright as day in the house," and he says "We eat so early," and she says "You can't eat late, not with your stomach," and he says "You're no better," and she says "At least I can still have spicy foods, if I actually liked spicy foods and you could eat them, too," and he says "Listen, the more I think of it, the more I think I could scrape enough together that one of us could go," and she says "By plane?" and he says "Maybe by train, or bus. Jim could drive one of us into Springfield, to the bus station. I don't know how long it'd be by bus, but that's an option," and she says "Then you should go," and he says "No, it really ought to be you," and she says "Not with my foot problems," and he says "Take the cane," and she says, "Even with the cane I'd slow everybody up," and he says "If it's you who goes, Frank'd certainly put you up, how could he refuse you?" and she says "Nobody ever said he'd refuse either of us," and he says "I'm just saying, you'd have a place to stay, and he could help you, or somebody would," and she says "I really think it should be you who goes," and he says "Why?" and she says "She was closer to you," and he says "How do you get that?" and she says "Well, she was, at least that's how it always felt to me," and he says "That's not the way it was at all, or are you just saying that because you don't want to go?" and she says "It's not a matter of not wanting to go, although it's something I never really considered or thought about, because it's just not the way things usually happen," and he says "Yeah," and she says "And what are you going to do here alone? Suppose you fall again?" and he says "Suppose I don't," and she says "Suppose you do," and he says "I've been very careful, even you have to admit that," and she says "Yes, but even when you're very careful something could happen, especially in the bathroom after you take a bath," and he says "I won't bathe until you get back," and she says "Lovely," and he says "Even if you were here and I did fall you'd have to call somebody anyway. You can't lift me, even if I have lost a little weight," and she says "You've lost more than a little weight. You're shrinking," and he says "I'm not as hungry as I was, and I'm not shrinking," and she says "When was the last time you tried on your suit? Go put it on, you'll see how much smaller you've become. Try it on anyway, if you're going," and he says "I'm not going, I'm not leaving you alone for two days. Let's drink this."

They look at the framed photo above the spinet. In the photo, she's wearing a pale blue dress and the pearl earrings her mother left her. He's wearing a brown suit and a wide brown necktie, his few remaining hairs carefully brushed over his scalp. Suzy stands between them, flashing a smile, her hair in braids. He says "Look how young," and she says "I think I still have that dress," and he says "I wish I still had some of that hair," and she says "Grass doesn't grow on a busy street," and he says "I wouldn't say that street was ever really so busy," and she says "Don't put yourself down," and he says "I don't think I ever noticed how crooked her teeth were," and she says "She got them fixed, later," and he says "Oh? Did I know that?" and she says "I don't know if you knew that," and he says "We should do this upstairs," and she says "What?" and he says "We're drinking a toast to her, right?" and she says "I hadn't thought of that, but you're right, that's a good idea," and he says "Only let me put the liqueur back in the jar, it'll be easier to carry, and you can carry the glasses, that way we both have one hand free for the banister."

He goes to the kitchen, pours the liqueur into the jar, brings the jar and glasses to her, hands her the glasses, and says "Now take it easy," and she says "You go first," and he says "No, you go first," and she says "You get so irritated with how slow I take the stairs," and he says "I've never," and she says "Just go, I'll meet you up there," and he says "I'll stay behind you, that way if you lose your balance I can break your fall," and she says "If that happens, I'm likely to knock you down, too, and we'll both break our necks, that'll be a nice picture for whoever finds us, both of us dead at the bottom of the stairs with booze all over us," and he says "Come on, come on, just go. I don't know why this is such a big deal all of a sudden, we walk up and down these stairs every day."

They go upstairs. Their bedroom to the left, Suzy's old room to the right, the bathroom central, down the short hall. They go into Suzy's old room. She says "Funny, coming up here I kept thinking 'Suzy's room' when it's really the guest room, although I can't recall ever having a guest in here," and he says "My mother, the week before she died," and she says "Oh, yeah," and he says "This house is too small," and she says "Now why in the world would you say something like that?" and he says "It just came to me," and she says "You've never complained before. Nor I, for that fact," and he says "Not true. There was that summer before Suzy went to high school you had me take you and her around to look at bigger places in Chatham," and she says "I'd forgotten that," and he says "And then you kept saying how everything would be too big for us, and too expensive," and she says "They were ugly houses," and he says "I don't remember that," and she says "Let's have the brandy," and he says "Liqueur."

He fills both glasses, hands one to her. They look around the room. Narrow bed, naked mattress. Simple, broad bureau. Oval rug of dull, red shag. One of his mother's old dining room chairs, the last of the set to survive. He says "She took everything else," and she says "Who?" and he says "Suzy. Who else would I be talking about?" and she says "I should put sheets on that bed," and he says "You used to," and she says "Well, I guess I just got out of the habit," and he says "Well. To . . . Suzy," and she says "To Suzy."

They drink. He says "Seem off to you?" and she says "Off?" and he says "Sour," and she says "It's supposed to be sour," and he says "I guess what I mean is does it taste like it went bad?" and she says "How would I know? It's been a million years since I had a taste of it." He pours himself another glass and says "Don't look at me like that. I can handle another ounce of this stuff," and she says "I'm not saying a word."

He drinks. They look around the room. She looks at him. "I'll call Jim Cloyd." She leaves.

He puts his glass down on the bureau, thinks, and opens one of the sock drawers. It's empty. He opens the other. A black button in a small plastic bag slides forward. He shuts both drawers. He runs his hand across the bureau, comes up with dust. He looks out the window, down into the small brown yard. He runs a hand along the sloping wall next to the bed. The wallpaper feels bubbly. He tries to smooth it out.

She returns. She says "I just got off the phone with Betty, she says Jessie's having a baby and she and Jim are driving up in the morning to stay with her a couple days," and he says "Which one's Jessie? Their eldest?" and she says "No, that's Patti," and he says "Where's Jessie live?" and she says "Beardstown," and he says "Boy or girl?"

and she says "Betty didn't know," and he says "Strange," and she says "That's because Jessie didn't want to know, just wanted a healthy baby," and he says "Good for them," and she says "So Jim's out," and he says "Well, that settles that."

The Big Book of Sounds

My Pop told me at one time or another (I was a kid, that's for sure), he told me, The reason people get in trouble is because they want to do things that can't be done, they can't help it. I didn't say anything and he said, You don't understand. I told him I didn't. My Pop looked at me then and said, You will when you're older and by then it'll be too late. And then he went back to his oatmeal.

The trouble with D.D. began either when she told me about her book or when we started shacking up because it made sense. D.D. was always over and I didn't blame her as her place was a crapbox. D.D. brought everything she had and I had room for it. The books everywhere added or so I thought a classy touch to my place but I guess plants would've been better not that D.D. or me have any interest in plants and would probably just let them die. So D.D. shows up and she's unpacked and there's all these books and she would write standing up which was great because I don't have a desk I use the kitchen table when I do the bills. Maybe trouble isn't the word I keep thinking of my Pop. Things were different is all.

My Pop liked a can of beer when he got home from work and told me at one time or another I was a kid that I know he told me, A can of beer when you get home settles you. My Pop could belch like a buzz saw you could hear him all over the house and he was proud of that. My Ma I remember wasn't so thrilled.

I come home one afternoon and open a can of beer and D.D. asks me to belch. I told her I couldn't just up and belch let me finish the can. She tells me to hurry so I hurry and finish and I let out a wreck my Pop would've been proud of and I'm laughing after it and D.D. is squealing with delight and then I see she was taping it. I ask her what gives and she tells me her editor wants her to write *The Big Book of Sounds*. I say, Oh. Then I say, What the hell does that mean. D.D. tells me it's what it says it is. *The Big Book of Sounds*. All the sounds a human being can make. I ask her who she thinks is going to buy a book like that and she tells me that's not her problem. I get another can of beer and sit down and tell her that's a hell of a way to start a book with me letting fly with one of my Pop's specialties and she tells me it's only the tip of the iceberg. I can see she's excited about it and so I say nothing more and turn on the television.

Both my Pop and my Ma didn't care much for D.D. when first I brought her by the house but they're both dead now and anyway I saw what they meant but D.D. was for me. All my Ma would say was, Oh she's very polite, or, Oh she's an interesting girl, and that was it. Whenever my Ma started saying something with that Oh you could tell that what she was about to say wasn't really what she wanted to say or was thinking of saying. That's why when at the end when she was in the hospital and I came and sat with her and one of the last things she told me was, Oh you were a fine boy, I knew I wasn't and I let it pass only I wish she hadn't've died the same day. This wasn't too long after my Pop had died and so I had nobody but D.D. and my brother Quinn who nobody ever heard from up in wherever he was

Montana or something. Anyway neither my Pop nor my Ma thought much of D.D. probably because she's a writer and wears glasses and wears skirts a lot. My Pop never said anything except once after D.D. had gone home after supper with us maybe an hour later my Pop told me, I always liked a girl who wore jeans because you can admire her ass and it's acceptable whereas girls with skirts well they're hiding stuff. He was watching the television when he said it probably to make it seem like he was commenting on something on the television but I knew better.

D.D. has this standing desk she made herself because she says when you buy a standing desk it's real expensive and they are I figured I'd get her a real one on Christmas but I looked online and there's no way. Hers was real sturdy anyway she did a good job on it. D.D. went everywhere with her tape recorder and I told her to get something digital nobody makes tapes anymore and she told me she had a stash she could just tape over whatever she had because all that stuff is on CD now anyway and I didn't say anything after that. She'd stand at her desk and write things down. One night she cleared her throat over and over again and I asked her was she sick and she said no and kept on clearing her throat. I threw a throwpillow at her to get her to shut up then and she told me, You know it doesn't come out the same every time. She looked excited and I said maybe she should move her desk into the bedroom so's the television wouldn't bother her. So she did. And I could still hear her.

My Pop told me at one time or another I was a little older then I think maybe junior high he told me A was what he wanted from me but he'd be happy with C so I got C's. He looked at every report card I brought home and read it like it was the TV Guide he would just look and look and he always said the same thing he'd say, I wonder

whose bright idea it was to leave out the E. He'd say this every time
and I never had an answer. He told me, They give you an A a B a C
a D but not E they skip right to F isn't that weird. I was starting my
smartass time at that time and I told him E would mean Excellent
and in that case you'd have to put it before A and then what would
A mean because there's nothing better than Excellent and he would
always tell me I might have a point there and then he'd sign the
report card and that was it for the night.

D.D. starts in making me her guinea pig always coming up with
a piece of paper and asking me to read what I saw. I'd read but it
wouldn't make any sense and she'd tell me to read it out loud and I
couldn't and she'd tell me to sound it out as best as I could and all the
time her tape recorder was running. I'd sound it out as best I could
and she'd get upset and excited at the same time and tell me, That's
not it at all that's nothing like what it was for me. And then she'd
go back to the bedroom and I'd go back to the television and get to
thinking I should take her out for a steak or something and then
we'd go over to Manetti's where they served everything.

We'd get our food and D.D. was always listening and loved it when
we went during the crowded times and we were shoved in among
other couples and long tables of families or friends. She was always
listening and asking me, Did you hear that did you hear that did
you hear that, and of course I heard everything but wasn't listening
so I didn't know what the that was that was making her so eager.
She'd take a break from listening and tell me, There's sounds people
make when they're talking and sounds people make when they're
listening and sounds people make when they're talking and eating
and sounds people make when they're first eating and sounds people
make when they probably don't think they're making a sound isn't

that fascinating. And then she would get depressed by dessert and I'd tell her to cheer up and she'd tell me, I'm only just beginning to realize the enormity of my task.

My Pop told me at one time or another I think when I was really little he told me, Never say anything you shouldn't say and you'll live a long and happy life. I didn't say anything and he said, Good boy.

The time comes when there's paper everywhere. I ask D.D. if she needs help organizing all of the paper and she tells me she doesn't know how to organize it yet and could I take off my shoes in the house and that was fine with me. She buys a digital recorder finally which she says is voice activated and it's neat there's a little red light on top that blinks on when you talk into it or somebody says something or anytime there's any sound at all. D.D. brings it to bed and tells me to just act natural and so it's on when we're fucking and she's totally into it wanting to do everything including stuff she'd never tried before and we have a good two weeks.

I come home and pop a beer and take off my shoes and find her crying a little at the front window and ask her what's wrong and she tells me, There's English and there's French and there's German and there's Dutch and there's Spanish and there's Russian and there's Swahili and there's Japanese and there's Chinese and there's Bulgarian and there's Gaelic and there's Hindu and there's Portuguese and I ask if she wants me to talk to her editor and she says no. She tells me she's collected forty-six variations of Hmm and says the problem is not so much transcribing the forty-six variations of Hmm as it is indicating what each variation means. There's the Hmm that's puzzled and a Hmm that's bemused and a Hmm that's troubled and a Hmm that's frustrated and a Hmm that's curious and she goes on and on telling me all forty-six and when she's done I say Hmm and she cries a little more and makes a note and says, Forty-seven.

My Ma would say to me, Oh it's not that, and, Oh I'm sure you'll figure it out, and, Oh I guess it's all for the best, and this was all before I figured out what that Oh meant. She didn't say Oh all the time before she said something to me or to my Pop or about one of her sisters or one of Pop's friends but she said it often and I wonder where she learned it. My Gramma I don't remember her too well because she was dead by the time I started first grade but I do remember I can still hear Gramma saying Here all the time just one word. Here handing me a cookie. Here helping my Granpa with his suspenders. Here passing the bread. Here feeding her blind poodle Here giving my Ma some money. Gramma didn't say anything much to my Pop not even Here. My Pop didn't say anything to her and even less to Granpa. My Ma would say to my Pop, Oh he likes you fine, and, Oh you're imagining things she always has a lot to do. I do remember the one time my Ma said to my Pop she told him, If you'd only waited it'd all be different, and then I knew she meant something but as I was young then I couldn't have been more than seven or eight as I was little then I didn't know what was meant by that only that she hadn't said Oh before she said it.

D.D. and I have a discussion that began as a joke a joke on my part. I told her it makes no sense to call it *The Big Book of Sounds* since it looks like it's going to be big so why not just call it *The Book of Sounds* and you should've seen the look I got but I kept going. People will see it's a big book so why be redundant. D.D. says to me, And where'd you learn that word, and that was enough to stop me because D.D. just didn't do that she never said things like that to me. I tell her it's a joke and she tells me it's not a very good joke and I tell her all right then it was just supposed to cheer her up and she tells me she doesn't need cheering up she needs she doesn't know what she needs and I tell her I'm going to talk to her editor because it's clear to me that *The Big Book of Sounds* is making her very unlike herself I mean aside from her aching back from standing and writing all day. D.D. tells me don't talk to her editor it's not his fault it's hers. And she tells me.

The Big Book of Sounds is my idea. I don't know where I got the idea. I was sitting with my editor and we were making fun of other people's books and crazy ideas for things to write about and he said one might as well write a book that describes all the different kinds of air and I said that's too easy because you can you can do that. And then I said what would really be a challenge is a book describing all of the sounds we make and every possible sound we could make and maybe even speculate on all the sounds we might make. And my editor laughed and said it'd be called *The Big Book of Sounds* and then he said, That's impossible. And while he was laughing I was thinking maybe it's not so impossible what if you could just by listening to yourself and everyone you meet what if you could write down all the sounds and he said then it would be just a big book of vowels and I said no there'd be consonants as well and he said he doesn't publish phonetics. Then I said to him because I got really excited I said no it would not be phonetics it would be all the sounds we make and also the sounds we make and what we mean by them so it would be a book to read aloud and a book to read at the same time. And he stopped laughing and he said, If you write it I'll publish it.

When she was done telling me this I asked her how far she was and she didn't say anything she just looked around the place at all the stacks of paper and I looked too. Practically everything was covered with piles of paper except my recliner in front of the television and standing there in looking at all of it I saw how much had piled up how deep she was how deep we were in this book and all she said then was I've barely scratched the surface. I looked at the mess I really, really looked at it and although I wasn't D.D. I tried to see it as D.D. was possibly seeing it and I told her all we needed was a bigger place. I went over to a stack of paper on the dining room table and picked up the top sheet and I looked at what she had written and I read what she had written I read it aloud. I read the next page aloud. I read the next page aloud. I read the next page aloud. I looked over at D.D. in her scarf-like skirt and her tight top and her mound of curly hair with the pencil sticking out and her delicate glasses and she told me to go on.

My Pop told me at one time or another no I know for sure it was the day he had the accident the day the last time I saw him not knowing it was the last time I would see him he told me, You can only do so much. I didn't say anything and he said, You don't understand. I told him I didn't and he didn't say anything for a short time and I thought that would be the end of it but then he told me, You can do anything and you can do everything and you can only do so much and while all of that is true you can only do so much for everyone and yourself and nothing is impossible if you have the time. I remember saying to him then I remembering finding my own voice then I remember I told him, So it's all about time, and he seemed surprised to hear me and he didn't say anything for a moment. My Pop smiled then and that was a good time it was always a reward that smile and my Pop told me, No it's not all about time not time only but maybe when you're older you'll understand. I told him, But then it'll be too late, and he didn't smile then he told me, Maybe it won't.

I read the next page aloud. I read the next page aloud. D.D. asks me, Do you understand. I tell her then, Oh yes, and I mean it oh yes I mean every word.

Acknowledgments

for my dear friend Stefanie Sundstrom Freeman, who read them first and read them best
and
for my family: Donald and Arlene Steinhagen, Donna Steinhagen Roth, and Steven Steinhagen

My sincerest thanks to the following print and online literary journals and their fiction editors for the initial publication of the following stories: "The Big Book of Sounds" in *The Atlas Review*; "Billy, Elaborated" in *Cloud Rodeo*; "Blue Tangle" in *Zest Literary Magazine*; "A Brief Survey of Faulty Contraception" in *Coup d'Etat*; "Certain Elements Combined" in *Gambling the Aisle*; "The Cruel Weddings of Ivy Lockton" in *Priceless Pennies*; "Division of New Hope" in *Four Ties Lit Review*; "Empathetics" in *Waxwing*; "Essential Knowledge" in *Barrelhouse*; "Husband Technique" in *Up the Staircase Quarterly*; "How to Handle the Educated" in *Pretty How Town*; "The Wind Catalog" in *The American Reader (as "I Want This Always")*; "Lasting" in *The Subterranean Review*; "Loami" in *Sou'wester*; "The Newly Discovered Unequivocal Origin of Baseball" in *Green Briar Review*; "Pamachapuka" in *Bodega*; "Score" in *Stoneboat*; "The [Some Girls] Assignment" in *Cloud Rodeo*; "Tour of Nothing" in *Serving House Journal*; "The Unreturned" in *matchbook*.

179

Lastly, my deepest gratitude to Gina Keicher and Diane Goettel, who made me see things I hadn't seen and understand things I hadn't understood.

Photo: Noah Simon

Jon Steinhagen is the author of the story collection *The Big Book of Sounds* (Black Lawrence Press, 2016). A Chicago-based author, playwright, songwriter, and actor, he was educated at DePaul University and Elmhurst College. He is a member of the Dramatists Guild of America and Chicago Federation of Musicians, and is currently a Resident Playwright at Chicago Dramatists; his stage works have been produced throughout the country, particularly the plays *Blizzard '67, Successors, Devil's Day Off, ACES, Dating Walter Dante*, and *The Analytical Engine*, and the musicals *The Next Thing, The Teapot Scandals*, and *Inferno Beach*. He has received four Joseph Jefferson Awards and ten Nominations for his work in Chicago theater as playwright, composer/lyricist, musical director, and actor. He is a past winner of the Julie Harris Playwriting Award and Clubbed Thumb Biennial Commission. His stories have appeared in publications such as *The American Reader, SmokeLong Quarterly, Wigleaf, Barrelhouse, Midwestern Gothic, Monkeybicycle, The Minetta Review, Waxwing, The Atlas Review, Sou'wester, East Coast Review*, and *Stoneboat*.